DIRTY DEEDS

A JAMES GAFFNEY CRIME THRILLER

ARMAND ROSAMILIA

Dirty Deeds

A James Gaffney Crime Thriller

Armand Rosamilia

Cover by Jack Wallen

JackWallen.com

Rymfire Books

http://armandrosamilia.com

Print Edition February 2016
eBook Edition January 2016 via Kindle Press

Dirty Deeds
A James Gaffney Crime Thriller
Armand Rosamilia

Special Thanks

to Shelly, who knew I could write this book and
nudged me gently to keep writing.

Billie Higgs, who beta read the book and made me
realize I had something special here.

Kindle Scout crew, for believing in this book enough
to accept it.

ONE

I get paid large sums of money to kill children.

I'll let that horrific sentence sink in before I tell you what I *really* do for a living.

More specifically, I move children from horrific situations with parents, guardians, and wicked people and place them with someone who will watch over them. Take care of them. Not want them dead.

How and why do I do this? We'll get back to the nitty gritty in a bit. For now...

"How much money to kill my daughter?"

I frowned and stared at the man. Without an answer, I walked to his office desk and sat down in the guest chair, and motioned for him to join me. I put my satchel on the floor within easy reach.

He took his time, trying to seem casual, walking around his desk and dropping into his chair.

I notice things.

A picture of his daughter was on the filing cabinet to my right. His hands were shaking and he couldn't make eye contact. He was sweating despite the air turned down low, and when I'd first walked into his office, I noticed his secretary was not at her desk.

John Caruso was one of the big shot lawyers in Philadelphia, but I would be stupid not to do my job and figure out the background of a potential client before we met. This guy had a couple of red flags and I was going to have my due diligence with John before we went any further.

I chuckled without humor and sat up in the chair. "If I'm not mistaken, you just asked me how much to kill your daughter?"

He nodded, his hands on the desk. When he moved his right hand to his phone on the desk he stopped, his hand shaking.

John was wearing a dress shirt. It most likely cost as much as my entire wardrobe. Especially what I was wearing. He was sweating so badly I could see his chest hair through it.

Me? I was calm and casual.

In the movies, the killer is always dressed smartly. Expensive Italian suits. Diamond-studded watch. Shoes like butter and worth the cost of a Porsche.

I was wearing a pair of jeans I'd bought at Wal-Mart, a black t-shirt that came in a pack of three, and boat shoes. Very comfortable, but not butter-comfortable. The most expensive thing I wore was the gold chain and cross around my neck, a gift from my deceased mother.

The pen on this guy's desk cost more than everything I had on even if you added in the cash from my wallet. I was sure his phone had every app imaginable to mankind and he didn't worry about his monthly bill.

"Don't play with me, Mister Aaron. You know exactly why you're here," John said. He sat up and his hands stopped shaking.

I knew the look on his face. He thought he had me. This little weasel thought he was back in control.

I turned my head and looked around the room. When I turned back to him he looked confused.

"I need water. Is there any way, before we begin the transaction that will change your life, you can get me a glass of water?" I asked.

"Uh... sure. I have bottled water."

I smiled and tried to fake warmth for this snake. "Actually, a tall glass of water is better. I don't even need it cold. I just need a lot of water." I touched my lips. "I get very thirsty doing this. You understand, right?"

"I have tap water," he said.

"Perfect."

John nodded and went out of the office and into his bathroom.

I scooped up his phone and sliced my finger across it, unlocking it quickly. These big shots were all the same: they'd spend thousands of dollars on home security but set their passwords to their computers so an eight year old could crack it, and never put anything safety-wise on their cell phone. I wasn't tech-savvy at all, but I'd paid a lot of money to learn the tricks I needed to learn over the years. I knew enough to keep me from getting backed into a corner or caught doing something stupid.

I found what I was looking for but didn't bother doing anything with it. I knew the score now.

John returned with the water and I sat up. I'd put his phone back but made sure it was moved half a foot to the right, away from him.

He noticed it right away and looked like he was about to run.

I put a finger to my lips and stood, taking the glass of water and taking a sip.

John didn't move.

The side of his mouth twitched when I picked up his cell phone.

"I think we got off to a bad start, Mister Caruso. You mistook me for someone else. Someone bad. I was contacted by a friend of a friend of a friend. This is how this happens and gets me in your office," I said. I sat back down and put the phone next to my glass of water.

I motioned for him to sit and I picked up my satchel from the floor on my side, keeping eye contact with the lawyer so he didn't bolt.

"I am selling this and I was told you had money for the purchase," I said and produced a 1973 Topps Mike Schmidt rookie baseball card, sealed and graded Gem Mint. Perfect 10. "You won't find this card in a better quality than this. Make me an offer I can't refuse."

John looked confused as he stared at the baseball card in my hand.

"I didn't invite you to my office to buy a damn baseball card," he said.

I picked up his phone with my free hand.

"Then I'm sorry for wasting your time. I really thought I was here to sell you a Schmidt rookie. I figured since we're in Philadelphia and you're obviously a hometown fan, it made sense to me. My bad. I'll be on my way," I said and stood, dropping his phone into the glass of water.

John panicked and tried to grab the glass but I pulled it away. I wanted to make sure it stayed in as long as possible. Not that it would do anything other than destroy his expensive phone. It was my own personal screw you to this jerk, who thought he was smarter than I was.

I yanked the phone out and spun it across the room, where it smashed against the wall.

"Oh no, I am so sorry. I will buy you a new phone. Is it broken?" I asked, running to it and *accidentally* stepping on the screen. It cracked. They didn't make them like they used to, right?

I could see he was getting pissed and about to say something really stupid. I turned, grabbed his arm, and pulled him to me. When I stared into his eyes he stopped and anger was replaced by fear.

"You got your wires crossed. I sell baseball cards. That's it. I don't know what you're talking about. You want to kill your daughter? I should go to the police, you sick bastard. Anyone who tries to pay someone to have someone killed, especially a child, deserves to die themselves. I hope, someday, you get what you deserve," I said and pushed him away.

I grabbed my satchel and walked out of his office, slamming the door behind me.

My instincts had saved me again but I was far from in the clear. I knew what was going to happen now.

As soon as I got outside there were lights in my eyes, armed police officers and men in black suits, and I was tossed to the pavement. It wasn't the first time and it wouldn't be the last, either.

They searched me, the FBI agent taking the lead disappointed I didn't have a weapon on me. I knew better. I didn't even carry a pair of tweezers.

I was put into the back of a squad car without a word and driven away. I didn't bother telling anyone they'd forgotten to read me my rights. They knew exactly what they were doing.

I'd been in this spot before. A lot worse, in fact. They had nothing on me and I wasn't going to slip like you saw in bad TV and movies. Not happening.

I enjoyed the ride. I'd flown into Philly so quickly I hadn't had a chance to see the city. Now, I watched it from the back of a police car.

* * * * *

It was Reggie Keane again.

Twenty years ago, when I'd first come onto his radar, he was a detective in the NYPD. He'd only been in a few years and was looking to make a name for himself. Since he'd almost nailed me in Spanish Harlem in 1996, he'd had an unhealthy obsession.

I called him Captain Ahab, which drove him nuts. I was his Moby Dick.

Agent Keane spread his stack of files on the table between us, not making eye contact just yet. It was always the same move from him: he'd try to disarm me with a lame look.

As soon as he looked up, going for his best DeNiro, I winked at him. He was flustered, as usual.

"Is there a reason I'm here, with you, again?" I asked. I leaned back in the chair and nodded at the two Philly cops standing near the door. "Am I a threat to you, Reggie? I don't even carry a weapon. You know all of this."

I was sure half a dozen FBI cronies were on the other side of the glass, taking notes. I knew most of them by face if not by name after all this time.

I was getting too old for this game, though. Keane was getting desperate. He was probably getting close to retirement age and needed to close the books on me before he got his pension, gold watch and was put out to pasture.

"I have a few questions to ask you," Reggie said.

"Sure, go ahead. I have a plane to catch in an hour, but I'll try to help in any way I can," I said. I didn't have a plane to catch. I gave him the line every meeting so he could bust my chops for two hours and feel like he'd accomplished something as insignificant as having me miss a plane back to wherever he thought I was going.

After this distraction, I was headed up the road to Manhattan to a sports card show. If he'd done even a bit of homework he would've known it.

Keane smiled. So predictable. "I think you're going to miss your flight… where are you headed now? I have sightings of you in Chicago, San Diego, Atlanta, Boston and Dallas in the last year."

He didn't mention Jacksonville or Newark, but he'd made my home in Chicago since our last talk. I'd make a note to have Marisa clear and sell it before the end of the year. What a shame. I was starting to like the summers in Chi-town.

"I am a legitimate businessman. I pay my taxes. I vote. I try to buy U.S. goods when possible. I recycle, too. If you're trying to shake me down in front of the Philly cops or your buddies in the FBI listening in, forget it." I smiled and leaned forward. "I told you the last time you tried to get a bribe out of me, and I'll tell you again: I'm doing nothing wrong, and there are real bad guys out in the world you need to concentrate on. Stop asking me for money. You might need a new job if you can't seem to get your mortgage paid on time."

Keane was getting hot and I was enjoying this, but I knew I needed to pull back. It was on the tip of my tongue to mention his cheating wife and the divorce papers signed a few days ago. I knew I was nothing more than a distraction right now. I felt sorry for Reggie, too. He wasn't a bad guy. He was doing his job and he did it quite well. He'd risen in the FBI ranks like a bullet (pun intended) but I was the obstacle keeping him from the big time.

"I know exactly why you're in Philadelphia," Keane said.

"I thought I was selling a Mike Schmidt rookie card." I turned to the two cops. "You guys get to go to Phillies games? I imagine with how bad the team is they let you in for free, right?"

Both cops tried their best not to snicker.

Keane opened a folder he'd had his hands on as if it would make for a dramatic move and I'd tremble in my seat.

He pulled the top page from it and smiled. "You know what this is?"

"All the cases you never solved because you're too busy with me?"

"No," Keane said and his voice cracked. I had him. "This is a thread we pulled off a message board three days ago. Mr. Caruso was talking to a Mr. Aaron, who set terms to kill his daughter at quarter of a million dollars. Does this ring a bell?"

"I know who Caruso is. The lawyer who flaked out when he saw how gem mint the Schmidt card was. I have no idea who Aaron is. Maybe another lawyer in his firm?"

I made a mental note to have Marisa wipe the message board clean. It was no longer safe. If Keane was smart he wouldn't have tipped his hand he had finally cracked the outdated means of communication between me and the evil in the world.

At the halfway point between forty and fifty, I wasn't tech savvy. I despised computers and only had a cell phone because I needed it for my life. It was an online world we lived in.

Back in the last part of the previous century I thought I had a firm grasp on technology. As I got older and the computers got smaller and smarter, I got lost. It was the same with music and TV and everything else. I freely admitted it. Marisa, who was still technically a teenager, spent most of her day wired on coffee and wired to the internet, making my job that much easier.

I needed to give the kid a raise.

"I'm not sure what you're insinuating. Should I get a lawyer?" I asked, knowing as soon as you mention a lawyer, the Feds and cops shut up.

Keane grinned. "I know a good lawyer. John Caruso. You just met him. He wants his daughter dead. Remember?"

Ahh. This wasn't a sting to catch me specifically. They'd been watching this idiot as he tried unsuccessfully to get his daughter killed. It probably hadn't been a trap until Keane got his mitts on the operation. He'd swooped in when he thought he'd finally get me. Instead of Caruso hiring a couple of undercover cops, who would simply arrest him, Keane had wired him for sound and given him a deal: help the FBI and they'd help you.

"Killing kids is a horrible thing. Hiring someone to do it is even worse," I said.

"How do you mean?" Keane asked, flipping through the papers in the folder.

"If you want someone dead, especially a family member, step up and do it yourself. You're an asshole for wanting to have someone dead to begin with, but your own kid? And you don't have the balls to do it yourself? I don't know what I just walked into in that law office but if you need me as a witness I'd be happy to help the FBI. He asked me point-blank if I wanted to kill his daughter for him. I thought I misunderstood," I said.

Keane stood and closed his file without showing me another page and more of his weak hand. He aimed a finger in my direction and I grinned when both cops took a step forward. This wasn't practiced or planned. Keane was going off-script and I'd gotten under his skin. Again.

"Don't think for a second you're fooling anyone. I know all of your aliases: Jones, Smoltz, Cox, Murphy, Spahn, Maddux, Niekro, Maddux, Glavine, Robinson and now Aaron. I don't know if they're random names or what, but I'm going to find out and take you down," Keane said.

"Uh, sir…" one of the police officers, a guy in his late twenties, put up his hand like he was in school. When Keane didn't bother asking him why he was interrupting but looked at the man, he got the hint to keep talking. "I know all those names. Baseball names, sir. If I'm not mistaken, they all played for the Atlanta Braves."

The cop looked at me, expecting me to answer.

"Not only are they all Braves, but I believe they are all players that had their numbers retired by the great franchise," I said. I looked at Keane and grinned. "I grew up in Atlanta, which I'm sure you knew. A simple Google search of the names would've gotten you this far."

Keane smiled. "I got you."

"I fail to see how me knowing about my favorite team makes me a criminal. If knowing sports is a crime, I'm guessing the cop here should go to prison for figuring out a bunch of names." I stood up. "Unless you're arresting me for something, I need to catch a flight. I'm not staying for coffee. If you ask me another question I'm going to lawyer up and not say another word."

"I know your name is James Gaffney. Your home address is listed in Atlanta. You do pay all your taxes on time and your side business of sports cards is rather lucrative. Hell, if you went legit and stuck to selling baseball cards you'd be a rich man," Keane said.

"I am a rich man because I sell baseball cards and nothing else," I said.

"Why have you killed all of these children?" Keane asked, dumping his folder on the table. Pictures of crime scenes spilled to the floor, but not one of them contained an actual body.

Like I said, I help these kids.

"I need to see my lawyer," I said and sat down. "I also need a cup of horrible Philadelphia coffee. Any chance Geno's is still open for a cheese steak sandwich?"

TWO

Marisa met me at the sports card show while I was setting up. She was nineteen but looked much older, and already I was getting annoyed at the old men setting up their displays around me and eyeing her like a piece of meat.

I knew she could take care of herself, though. She'd been in and out of foster care since running away from the first family I helped put her with.

She often asked who her real parents were, knowing I'd never tell or leave a paper trail for her to find. It didn't work like that.

Right now she was pissed at me.

"I'm seriously going to do the setup without you from now on. Give you an address and a target and tell you to get it done. You're taking risks you don't need to take, old man," Marisa said.

We had our philosophical differences over the way I handled my business. I learned to do it in person, to meet the man or woman who wanted to kill a child and commit them to memory. Someday I'd do something about each and every one of them.

Marisa was new school, where you did it all anonymously online. You couldn't be traced and the only way you got caught was by physically doing the dirty deed and something going wrong. Her argument was valid: why take so many risks when you no longer had to? But I'd been doing this long enough to know I had to do it this way for my own moral compass, as skewed as it was. I wanted to see these people in person, or at least as close as they'd let me. Someone responsible for these supposed deaths was going to be etched in my mind forever.

I knew if I ever decided to hang it up and pass along the knowledge and business to anyone it would be Marisa, and I knew she'd make quite a few drastic changes.

Hell, I reminded myself about all the changes I'd made as a cocky twenty-something in the 1990's. I'd updated the 1960's mentality for this work, and Marisa would update it to the 2020's. Every thirty years or so there'd be an improvement or two. As long as we saved children, who cared?

"I saw your buddy, Keane, outside. I had no idea he was such a memorabilia collector," Marisa said and helped me to put my table together. She was way more organized than I'd ever be. She kept begging me to let her inventory everything I owned but I wanted it to be a pleasant mystery. I still remembered opening packs of baseball cards in the mid-1970's and searching for the handful of cards I needed to make the complete set or add to my growing Atlanta Braves collection.

"He surprises me at times. I know he didn't follow me, and after I stopped his interrogation last night and asked for a lawyer, he let me go within an hour. A new record," I said. "Is he getting better in his old age?"

"He got lucky. What's the stupid saying you always use? Sometimes even a blind horse can find water?" Marisa smirked. Her long blonde hair was up in a ponytail and she wore no makeup, but she was still attractive. Don't get me wrong, I was no pervert. I was more than twice her age and she truly felt like my daughter. But I needed to protect her from a room filled with dudes who would hit on her. I could only imagine what would happen if she went to a nerd convention.

"He knows about Chicago and how to get in touch with me now, too," I said.

"I have Irwin selling the Chicago place this week. You might lose a few bucks but it will be a loose thread neatly tied up. I've destroyed the server for the message board and will start up a Facebook page for it soon," Marisa said.

"You're going to post on the biggest social media outlet I'll take your money and kill your kid?" I asked. "That makes no sense."

"Hide in plain sight. Remember that gem of a saying you used to hit me with all the time when you caught me trying to run away? We're still mostly word of mouth for rich depraved people who know what to look for online when they want to do something vile. Unfortunately, returning customers have now moved up to about twenty percent of our clientele. I guess once you've paid to have your kid killed, you want to kill them all," Marisa said.

"I hope Keane doesn't make a scene. It'll be bad for business." These big card shows would attract a ton of buyers as well as guys trying to unload a few things, but today I was in the mood to sell as much product as possible and fly out without having to worry about packing any of it.

The money didn't matter to me. It hadn't in a long time. This was more of a hobby than a way to pay the bills. Unfortunately, sick bastards who wanted me to harm their children paid for the multiple houses and my own card collections.

I was born in 1969 and became an Atlanta Braves fan at seven years old. I've been on the lookout for gem mint 1969 Topps cards and anything Braves I can get my hands on. Everything else gets sold.

I owned over a million non-baseball cards, stored in two warehouses, one on either side of the country: football, hockey, basketball, and miscellaneous stuff. I'd gladly trade it for every '69 Topps and/or Braves card in the world, although it was fun to build the sets one card at a time.

Marisa casually nodded her chin past me and I looked and caught the eye of the redhead setting up at the table next to me. She was pretty. About my age. Definitely staring at me. I'd seen her before at a few shows and I turned back to Marisa and told her to stop.

"Stop what?" she asked, trying to sound innocent and failing. "This is the third show in a row she set up next to or near you. It's not a coincidence. The last time she tried to talk to you and you blew her off."

"No way." I remembered, and she and I talked business for awhile. Her husband had died and left her with his collection, which she'd managed to build and begin selling at shows. She had some nice cards and I made a mental note to check out her Braves and 1969 offerings.

"Go talk to her. Ask a few questions. Live a little," Marisa said.

"I'm busy. This is work." I glanced over and the redhead smiled at me again as she continued to set up for the show.

I focused on the job at hand. I needed to concentrate on this card show and my near miss with Keane and why he was here today. I bumped into Marisa, who was trying to set a speed record for setting up my tables.

Marisa seemed antsy today.

"What's the matter?" I asked.

"Nothing," she lied. I could always tell like she could with me, when something was bothering the other.

"Out with it."

Marisa stopped moving product onto the table and smiled. "I had a date last night. It went great. He wanted to see me again right away but I told him I had work and would be out of town."

"First date?" I asked, trying not to act like a father but failing as bad thoughts raced through my head about this guy. "How old is he? Where did you meet?"

Marisa laughed. "Yes, our first face to face date. He's a couple of years older than me. Very mature. We met on a hacker message board about six months ago." She grinned. "He was a perfect gentleman."

"Good," I said.

"As for me… well…"

"Not funny," I said.

When we were done Marisa asked if I'd eaten. I hadn't. Despite really wanting an authentic cheese steak from Philly last night, I'd gone to McDonalds and crashed. This morning breakfast consisted of two cups of coffee made in my hotel room.

"I'm going to get you something delicious," Marisa said.

"Your idea of delicious is not even close to mine. I want meat."

"Meat is murder," Marisa said. Before I could finish she smiled. "Tasty, tasty murder. I know you too well."

"You can't throw my own lines back at me. Not fair. Seriously, I don't want a salad or tofu or anything natural. I want a greasy burger and some fries. I'll eat better when I get home," I said. She knew it was a lie and so did I. It was the game we played.

Marisa stared at my growing belly and sighed. "How old are you again?"

I shook my head and took out two twenty dollar bills from my pocket. "Here. Use this. I need some small bills."

"You do remember we're in New York City, right? What do you think I can buy with this?"

True. I handed her two hundred dollar bills. "Break these. I want the change back, and the two twenties."

"What twenties?" Marisa asked with a smile. I paid her quite well but she still treated me like I was her dad and made out of money. While I preferred to wear shorts and faded t-shirts, she wanted the nicer things in life. I wanted to eat greasy burgers and pass out watching the game.

Before we go any further, there are a couple of points I need to clear up.

Morally I do nothing wrong. No, I'm not a saint by any stretch. In my personal life I might've stolen a candy bar when I was a kid or lied to people or done typical kid stuff. I grew up in a bad part of Atlanta, where you did what you had to do. In my personal life I'd done worse things but that's for another time.

I'm talking about my job. The job where bad people pay me to do one of the worst things imaginable, and they don't care. I often wonder what it takes to set something like this in motion in their heads, but I don't want to stare too closely into this abyss.

Knowing I'm taking their money and saving the intended target is worth it to me. Marisa once asked, years ago, why I didn't take the money, save the child and then call in an anonymous tip or go back and kill the parent. It would be easy enough to do.

But I can't, because if word got out one of the jobs I was tasked with went south, I'd lose future clients and future children being saved. Simple as that.

Don't get me wrong… the money is good. Really good. Money isn't the only thing in this lifetime, though, is it?

"James?"

I didn't realize he was talking to me at first, deep in my thoughts and setting up displays for my cards. When I turned I sighed. It was Agent Keane again.

"I've often wondered if James was your real name. I guess I have my answer," Keane said.

"Funny, it says James on my birth certificate." Of course, it was a fake like everything else. There was no way Keane or anyone else was getting close to the real me. The old me, the life I grew up in and my family and name, are all gone now. Scattered on the wind like ashes, as the saying goes. I keep looking ahead.

"I'm going to find out what you're *really* doing one of these days," Keane said, staring at me with his hands in his pockets. He was staring and watching me set up my displays.

"What I'm *really* doing is earning an honest buck selling sports cards to guys who are trying to stay young or remember a better, simpler time in their lives," I said.

"I guess that's what it is for you: a connection to something you lost or never had?" Keane was grinning now. He thought he had me for some reason.

"Everyone collects something. Cards. Comic books. Matches. Stamps." I glanced at Keane to make sure he was still staring at me. "Drunk driving arrests. Ex-wives."

If Keane had been drinking anything he would've spit it out by the look on his face. I'd been saving that information for awhile and planned to use it when I was in a jam, but it was worth it. He had no idea I'd done my homework. He'd never done his.

"I hope you have all of your tax papers and licenses on you," Keane said.

"Actually, I do. I always check in with the people running the event to make sure they know everything is good. The two cops near the door behind me already know I'm legit, too. If you think you're going to bust my chops by making a scene I'd think twice about it." I smiled. "Up until this point you and I have done this dance on the up and up, haven't we? No cheap shots. No false arrests. No tossing cars and bothering friends and family. This is a professional and courteous relationship we have, Reggie."

"You're the one who brought up a DUI and ex-wives," Keane said.

"Ex-wives? You got more than one?" I asked, knowing he had two. Valerie was the first wife. They'd married early and it only lasted a year before she cheated with a guy Keane worked with. Sloppy divorce. She remarried and had two kids. Second wife, Linda, worked in D.C. for a senator and the affair was almost front page news, except there was a big payoff of quite a few people to keep it under the rug. I didn't think Keane had taken a bag of cash to shut up and sign the divorce papers, which was why his bank account was often in the red right before payday. Linda still worked for the cheating bastard senator.

"I think I underestimated you," Keane said.

And there it was. The light bulb had come on in his head and he was staring at me. I'd messed up. Arrogance was always my worst enemy. I'd ruffled his feathers and now he was pissed. He'd not make many more mistakes from this moment on, and Keane would do everything in his power to nail me. I'd made it personal and I felt like an idiot.

Marisa was back with a bag already crusted with grease. Delicious.

"If you'll excuse me, Agent Keane, I have to eat before the crowds get too unmanageable. Can I interest you in a Joe Namath rookie? I only have two and they'll go quickly in Manhattan."

Keane shook his head and looked at the greasy bag of food.

"You want some fries?" Marisa asked.

"I want to know where you went. I'm starving," Keane said.

While Marisa played nice and gave him directions I went back behind my tables. I needed to finish setting up and getting my stock into position. I was always paranoid someone would come by and not see what they were looking for and move on to the next guy and drop big money. I wanted everything out and in order so I could sell it.

An older man wearing a faded Atlanta Braves cap came over and adjusted his glasses, looking at the displays I had already set on the main table.

"You looking for something special?" I asked and remembered to smile.

"I don't see any Braves cards."

He didn't because I don't sell them, or 1969 Topps baseball cards. Yeah, I'm one of those guys: I break the cardinal sin of selling anything… I dabble in the merchandise myself.

"I don't sell any. I'm also a collector." I put up my hand when he started to tell me how it was done. "I'm not in this to make a million dollars. I'm actually doing this so I can buy Braves cards for myself. In fact, I am willing to pay high-end book value for any good card."

Now I had his attention. He might be a collector but he also knew a good deal when it was presented to him, and he was going through his doubles and extra cards in his head right now.

Keane was watching and I could tell he was fascinated. I think up until this point he thought this was a sham, a front for my illegal dealings. To see me in action, buying and selling cards, and knowing what I was talking about, was magical. To me, anyway. Marisa told me I was a boring old geek.

I slipped a business card into the man's hand. "Send me an e-mail with whatever you have. A picture would be nice, too. We'll make a deal. I'm here all weekend, too."

"I'll run home tonight and see what I have. I wasn't planning on coming back tomorrow, but maybe I will," he said.

"I look forward to seeing you," I said.

He looked at the business card and grinned. "James Gaffney. Why does that name sound familiar to me?"

I kept my smile and shook his hand. "Just a happy coincidence." Once again my arrogance had gotten the best of me. Of course I'd stolen the name from the former owner of the Boston Braves, who'd owned the club from 1912 until 1915 when he sold it to Percy Haughton, another name I'd used in the past.

Reggie Keane (definitely his real name) was smiling at me now. He was starting to piece a few things together and I knew I was in trouble.

When the old man walked away I thought for sure Keane would pounce, but instead he waved and said his goodbyes to Marisa.

He was smarter than he looked. Suddenly Keane was dangerous.

"Oh, by the way…" Keane said and stopped walking away, turning to face me.

He had something big and he was about to drop it on my head.

"Any chance you know a guy named Chenzo from New Jersey?"

"Isn't every Italian in Jersey named Chenzo?" I asked. I knew who he was talking about and I felt the weight falling from the sky.

"This Chenzo is unique. He's a reputed boss of The Family. He lost his kid about fourteen years ago. His wife went missing, too. Real shame. What a manhunt it was to find them. She was found with her throat slashed in the parking lot of Yankee Stadium. The son was never seen again, which is a real tragedy," Keane said.

"I remember reading about it in the paper." I'd taken the kid and set the little monster with a good family in Montreal. He was only four or five but already a terror. Chenzo couldn't handle his son and the wife was not only cheating with another Made guy but she was stealing coke and cash as well. Chenzo decided to wipe the slate clean and start over. The guy she was seeing was never found again, although I know her public assassination was a lesson for everyone. By the way, I didn't kill her. It wasn't my style and I wouldn't take money for it. If I was going to kill someone it would be personal and I'd do it for free.

"Funny thing about the son, who they called Little Chenzo: he would've turned eighteen this year. In fact… he did," Keane said.

"They found him alive? Great news," I said. I could feel a drip of sweat on my temple. This was bad. This was really, really bad.

"I'm sure Chenzo will be happy. The funny part is this entire time I assumed you'd killed the kid for The Family."

I'd assumed I'd gotten the kid far enough away and he'd be taken care of and nothing like this would ever happen.

I was in trouble.

THREE

It had been nearly seven months since the Caruso debacle, and I was starting to enjoy my freedom and life not having to plan another kidnapping. As far as my eyes and ears on the ground were concerned, Chenzo's kid hadn't made an appearance. I'd spent quite a bit of money to find out if it were true and so far all I'd gotten were unconfirmed sightings and rumors but nothing concrete. I even had a guy inside the organization I used for some of the harder cyber stuff, but Marco was too close to the Boss and I wasn't going to tip my hat I had anything to do with this.

So far it was an unconfirmed rumor. A rumor that would get me in trouble sooner than later.

It was only a matter of time before Chenzo and The Family called to set up a meeting and I wanted to get all my ducks in a row. I also needed to talk to the kid.

Tracing him back through my network is never easy, because it's purposely setup so no one can find information. When I need to find this information, however, it is just as hard to move up the line. I spend a lot of money to cut loose ends and pay the right people off to walk away or forget they saw something, and most of them have no idea it was my money greasing a palm and keeping them silent.

Marisa was busy trying to get as much intel as possible on the kid, who'd truly dropped off the face of the earth. I didn't know if a rival of Chenzo had the kid, or Chenzo had him stashed, or the FBI was even now questioning the kid, or an infinite number of possibilities, all bad for me.

Miami was too hot and a jaunt to the Keys before a flight to anywhere north was in the cards over the next week or so. I never liked to plan anything too far in advance. The fun was surprising myself.

Next month I'd be doing a card show in San Diego, a small one near the military base. Some of my best customers were Navy SEALs. You'd think they were all a bunch of adrenaline junkies, but some of them liked to relax and collect some cards.

Despite what I might have intimated, if I did more than one of these jobs a year it was a surprise. I'd once gone twenty-two months without a job about ten years ago, my longest stretch. The baseball cards kept me out of trouble and with a constant flow of money in and out.

Marisa was officially my webmaster for the buying and selling of the sports stuff, and she did an excellent job of it. Most days she talked way over my head with what she was doing when it came to online stuff. I just saw money adding to my bank account and every now and then I'd spend some or skim some off the top in cash and hide it. Old habits and all that shit.

My phone rang, waking me from a late morning nap. Yeah, I was officially getting old. It was Marisa.

"I think I located the son. He was found off the coast of Massachusetts about two hours ago. I paid off a detective and two uniformed cops who discovered the body on a beach. Matches the description. They can sit on it for twelve hours before they have to start the process," Marisa said.

"He drowned?"

"Technically. The four bullets in his body didn't kill him, but they would have eventually. They think he was in the water about six hours. Luckily he wasn't dumped into the ocean and drifted too far," she said.

"Whoever did it wanted the kid to be found," I said. This was a message, but I didn't know who it was for. Chenzo? Me? Something completely unrelated? Now, with the kid dead, I had no idea how I'd get information.

"I've located the address he was living right before this," Marisa said.

"Send it to me and book a flight."

"I already have. Check your burner phone," Marisa said. There was a pause on her end.

"What?"

"This kid, as you keep calling him... he wasn't much younger than me. I've figured out I was the first one you'd saved on your own. Was he the second?"

I hesitated. You never wanted to give out information that could come back later and bite you on the ass, or get someone else in a bad position if someone bad came looking for an answer. With Marisa I assumed she'd already figured out the answer to most questions she asked.

"Yes. Little Chenzo was the second job I did."

"He was named William. Will Black. He has a rap sheet a mile long. Drug addict. He's been living on the streets since he was twelve. Damn fine musician from what I've pieced together. He was a nightmare for the parents and they gave up on the kid. They let him go and never bothered to tell anyone. I think they somehow knew there was a problem with the adoption," Marisa said.

"I need their address as well," I said. Marisa did great work and I had no doubt I was ahead of everyone else so far. I was hoping the kid dying had nothing to do with the rumors of who he was, and it was a drug-related death. Maybe it would solve a few things if I could keep it under wraps and keep it quiet.

"There's another hitch," Marisa said.

"I'm listening."

"Sister Patricia had a visitor this morning. He asked way too many questions. He said he'd be back with a search warrant for her records," Marisa said.

"Damn Keane." He wouldn't find anything but Sister Patricia was getting older and I knew she had a few others helping her now in her advanced age. I knew I should've switched the adoption agency years ago, but I had a soft spot for the woman. I knew she'd taken care of my own move as a baby. I told you I wasn't all bad. But if someone she was working with now was privy to what I was doing or even suspected, they might slip and tell the FBI.

I guarantee there are people scratching their heads right now wondering why I just don't come clean to the Feds and explain what a wonderful thing I'm doing. I wish it were that simple.

I learned from my predecessor and mentor how it would really work: a lot of pissed off really bad people would come after me, and the government wouldn't be able to stop them. Hell, some of the government officials had been involved in this either as a payoff or, in a couple of cases, had a problem solved this way.

That would be a major can of worms opened. The other downside would be whoever stepped in to take my place (and there would always be someone to take your place no matter how unique your skill set was) and they'd actually kill little kids.

Think about it.

It would be far easier to let Agent Keane into my dirty little secret, but the ramifications were too great if he didn't play ball or thought he was helping by telling his bosses, who told their bosses, until it got to someone who I'd done a job for.

I couldn't take a chance.

Marisa filled me in on the pertinent information: the cops I needed to get to as soon as possible, followed by the slum Will was living in before he died, and then his adoptive parents to see what I could shake up.

So much for the Keys, but I was glad to be leaving Miami. I had nearly four weeks before I had to be in San Diego, and I thought I had enough time.

I packed a bag quickly and was through the lobby and outside into the oppressive heat just as the car to take me to the airport arrived. I made a mental note to thank Marisa again and give her another raise.

* * * * *

If I didn't know any better, I'd think Reggie Keane had been hustling me all these years, lulling me into a false sense of security before pouncing.

When I stepped off the plane in Boston, Reggie was waiting for me with a smile.

"What brings you to town, James?"

"Want to catch a Red Sox game. I haven't been to Fenway Park in a couple of years and since I have time to kill until my next card show, I decided to take a mini-vacation. What brings you to Boston?" I asked. I hoped he'd gotten lucky and someone had tipped him off I appeared on a flight when Marisa booked me and nothing more. If he was still in New York it would've been a much quicker jump to Boston to await my arrival.

"Same. I've never been to Fenway. How about I join you?"

I smiled. "I'll get the tickets and you get the beer and hot dogs. Sound fair?"

Reggie nodded. "The game starts at seven tonight. But I'm sure you already knew. What hotel are you staying at?"

"Eliot Hotel on Commonwealth," I said, knowing it was the best of the best. Over five hundred a night and more if you book last-second and have to make sure you get a luxury room.

Agent Keane smiled. "I need to get a room." He checked his watch. "It's three now. I'll pick you up at the hotel around six-fifteen."

"Great. I'm looking forward to it," I lied. I excused myself to get my luggage. Keane walked off but I could see the sloppy tail following my every move. He'd be easy enough to shake when I was ready.

I called Marisa and filled her in about Keane. She bought two tickets to the game on the third base side and told me the Tigers were in town. At least it would be a decent game on the field, and I'd have to bring my A game when talking with Reggie. This wasn't going to be a social visit and two longtime buddies catching a game and drinking a couple of beers. Frankly, I was impressed with Reggie for being so bold and inviting himself to the game.

I rented a car and immediately took off, losing my tail within two blocks. Boston was a great city to shake someone with the way the streets have been laid out, like a chaotic maze and no forethought to people getting around. I knew the city well and was heading east towards the beach and the cops, knowing I was going to cut it close if there was a glitch.

I broke a few speeding laws on the way and might have driven on the median at one point when the fast lane was too slow for my tastes, but I didn't get pulled over and I arrived at my destination ahead of my personal schedule.

Two cops stood over the covered body and when I announced myself and slipped both a crisp hundred dollar bill extra for their troubles, they let me see the kid.

He was dead. The last time I'd seen him was too long ago, and I had no idea if this was even him until the autopsy came back. I could see his waterlogged flesh on both arms had track marks, though. He was a junkie.

"When will you be doing the write-up?" I asked.

"As soon as you walk away we make the call. Do you know the kid or want to make a statement?"

"I wasn't here." I gave them both a business card. "Do me a favor: when you notify the parents and they say it's their son, I need to know they verified everything. Got it?"

Both cops nodded. They knew I'd give them a few more bucks for their trouble, too.

It might have been a wasted trip, but I didn't think so. The cops would stay close to the body and no one would mess with it. As soon as the parents claimed him I could have a chat with them.

I hadn't planned on staying in Boston but I'd get an early jump in the morning and drive to New York. I called Marisa and told her to book me a bogus flight back to Miami in the late morning. I'd eat the ticket but get Keane off my back.

Traffic was a bitch getting back into Boston but I made the hotel by five, parked and smiled when I saw my tail, waiting in the parking garage. He'd spent the last two hours sitting and stewing. I was sure he'd neglect to mention to Keane I'd shaken him with ease.

I had enough time for a quick shower and a change into a pair of well-worn jeans and a black t-shirt with my faded Braves cap for good measure. I was in Boston, where my favorite team had started, so I felt comfortable wearing it. I never bothered unpacking the cap when I was in Philadelphia or Queens. Those fans would pour a beer on your head.

By the time I got down to the lobby Reggie was waiting, watching the rich tourists or businessmen coming and going. He greeted me with a quick wave. I could see he was dressed casual for his style, with no tie on a button-down shirt and a pair of loose-fitting khaki pants. I could see he was unarmed, too. I knew I was no physical threat to him in his mind. He thought wrong, but it wasn't like I'd break his arm unless I had to.

Let's stop again so I can reset and fill you in on a few things: I'm in my mid-forties, like I already said. I'm a bit overweight, like Marisa loves to point out. I don't run unless absolutely necessary, and then usually for a pizza. I do all of my work by stealth and infinite patience when I'm working the job. I don't carry a gun even though I own quite a few. I'm not an assassin. I think I said it before, but I'll reiterate the point. I'm no killer, even though I have the greatest reputation for being one. But don't cross me, because there are those who've done it in the past and while I haven't killed anyone so far, the day was still young, as the saying goes.

Did I touch on this before? It sucks getting old.

FOUR

Another aside before we continue.

Sitting with Reggie, enjoying a cool summer night watching a baseball game and my mouth watering as I'm waiting for the hot dog guy to pass me a couple of good ones, I'm struck by the realization I'm not a calm as I've probably led some to believe.

If I'm acting like I'm as cool as the other side of the pillow, it's all an act.

Despite the hunger, my stomach was roiling for another reason. I was nervous. Even though Keane and I had an odd and civil relationship, I had no doubt he was trying to trip me up with every innocuous question or comment. He was trying to feel me out, and after the last couple of days I knew his bumbling Keystone Cops routine was his way of getting me off my guard. It had worked. I stepped right into the Caruso office and nearly got crushed because of my own arrogance.

Reggie Keane was in Boston for the same reason I was, and it didn't look promising for me. I could throw a ton of money at the problem but in the end, he had the badge and the right.

All I had was two delicious hot dogs and a cold beer, and baseball. I'd take it for tonight, but tomorrow I needed to move quickly. I shared a few hints about my past, most of them common knowledge he'd already know, and a few falsehoods to make him waste time checking to see if they were true.

By the seventh inning stretch we were talking more about baseball than trying to trip one another up, and I was starting to relax. My bad.

"I know you went and saw the kid on the beach. I know he's someone who is supposed to be dead, and I also know Chenzo isn't too happy about it," Keane said after singing along to Neil Diamond together and finishing our third beers.

I remained calm but I could feel the hot dogs trying to come back up in my stomach. I turned and looked for the beer guy or the hot dog guy or anyone who could distract me while I collected my thoughts, as jumbled as they were right now.

I had to give Reggie credit: he'd thrown me a curveball and I was about to swing and miss.

Instead, I said nothing. Like an idiot. I glanced at Reggie and he was smiling. He thought he finally had me.

I took his arrogance and used it to get back in the game. There was no way this snide bastard was going to get the best of me.

"I thought it was a friend of the family. Turns out it was just some drug addict washed up on the beach? Again, I know who Chenzo is, but so does half this stadium and we're not even in New Jersey right now. The guy is a thug and a menace. Not something I deal with, unless he wants to buy a Babe Ruth card. Even then I try to get someone between us to do the deal. Unfortunately, in both our lines of work, we deal with people who aren't necessarily good but they have money to spend," I said.

"They're running DNA on this kid as we speak. As soon as it comes in I'll get Chenzo to give up a sample as well. What do you think he'll say when his kid, who's been presumed dead for all these years, comes back?" Reggie was staring at me.

I turned back to the game just as Ortiz came up for the Red Sox.

"You're chasing butterflies again, Reggie. I thought we were actually bonding tonight."

Ortiz swung and missed a slider inside. You never wanted to test Big Papi.

"I need to know what your connection is to Chenzo. We've been trying to get this guy for years, and we always assumed he'd had his son killed. His alibi was way too convenient. With the wife butchered we thought it only a matter of time before the kid's body showed up in a landfill or at least blood evidence in a junkyard. Now this... I know you killed the wife. Why let the kid go?"

Next pitch to the batter was high and outside. Ball.

"I didn't do any of this. Don't you get it? The real killer of Chenzo's wife is still out there. It isn't like he doesn't have fifty guys who would gladly kill for him. I'm sure you know this." I watched a ball in the dirt to Ortiz.

"I'm getting closer. I'll nail you. Word on the street is Chenzo wants to see you. That isn't a coincidence, James. It would be really bad for you if Chenzo finds out the son has been alive this entire time and you've hidden him away for some odd reason. This kid is the heir to his illegal throne, and my gut tells me Chenzo ordered the hit on his wife and son all those years back. Did you go soft for some reason? See a little of the kid in yourself? Couldn't take killing another child?"

Ortiz took another swinging strike.

"You're barking up the wrong tree, Keane. If you had anything on me, *anything*, we wouldn't be sitting in this stadium eating hot dogs and drinking beer like old friends. We'd be at the nearest police station awaiting a flight back to FBI headquarters so you could parade me around the office after all these years," I said.

"I can't quite put a finger on you. Never could, as you know. You've run rings around me for years. Every big kidnapping has your name on it, though. I can feel it in my bones. Now I'm starting to wonder…"

Ortiz hit a mammoth home run to straightaway center field and the crowd cheered. I had to stand and give props to the man as well.

"You want another hot dog?" I asked Reggie when I sat back down. He was no longer making pretend he was watching the game.

"I want answers," Keane said.

"You're asking the wrong person," I said.

Keane shook his head. "Here's the funny part: every few months, maybe two or three times a year, a celebrity or drug lord or millionaire has a child kidnapped. Blood is spilled at the scene at times, and maybe a ransom note is sent or a mysterious phone call asking for millions. Nothing ever comes of it, though. While the police are chasing a phantom, the kid vanishes into smoke. Never to be heard from again. No shallow graves. No fingers sent in bloody envelopes in the mail. No follow-up ransom calls or money requests. It's all a sham, and I think I figured out what's going on."

I put my hands at my sides as I sat because I could feel them start to shake.

"Care to take a guess?" Reggie asked.

"You're doing pretty well up to this point. Why don't you keep babbling while I enjoy the last couple of innings?" I nodded to the hot dog guy, my new best friend, and put up two fingers. "You want another dog?"

"Sure," Reggie said.

I put up three fingers.

Reggie handed me a twenty dollar bill. "My turn to pay."

I didn't argue. He was busting my chops and getting way too close for comfort now. I needed Agent Keane to go away and let me do my job, but it interfered with his. One of us was going to walk away at the end of this story, and I needed to do everything in my power to let it be me.

"You're too quiet now. I think I struck a nerve," Keane said.

"No. When you actually have something worth listening to I'll comment. You're chasing ghosts. It would be great to say all those kids you've been searching for are alive and well and living on an island with Jim Morrison, Elvis, Amelia Earhart and Bigfoot in sin. But we both know the sad truth: people kill people, no matter what the age or race or anything else. In the end, no one is safe from a murderer. I'm surprised there aren't more of these celebrity kidnappings, to be honest. One or two a year isn't bad odds at all. I wouldn't worry too much if I were rich," I said.

"Aren't you, though?"

I shrugged. "I do quite well. My sports card wheeling and dealing is great. I can't complain. It allows me to take trips like this whenever I want without worrying about money. I've never been married and have no kids. I can come and go as I please. I'm living the dream," I said truthfully.

"It must be nice," Reggie said quietly. He was staring at the field but not watching the game. "I like you, James, or whatever your real name is. I really do. I wish I had the life you lead."

"Then work for me. I could always use a security detail when I move some of my bigger collections," I said impulsively. Yeah, I was thinking of buying him and being done with it. I knew even if he accepted, and I knew he never would, another FBI agent would pick up the pieces and the trail eventually. I could only buy his silence with a steady paycheck for so long, anyway. Reggie Keane wasn't a guy you could buy no matter what the cost was. I respected and hated him for it right now.

"You know I can't do it. I know you'll never admit to any wrongdoing and I'd be disappointed if you did, but you're involved in something very big and very bad. I'll figure it out and slap the cuffs on you. You're about the only thing keeping me from retiring, actually," Keane said.

"Which is why I call you Captain Ahab," I said.

"I'm a dinosaur in this business. I know it. If it wasn't for these missing kids I'd be long gone to Boca Raton, looking forward to the early bird specials," Reggie said.

"You said missing kids."

Reggie grinned. "Before this week I called them dead kids. Children you slaughtered for money, and still slept at night. Honestly, I feel better about you now. If it turns out you're only stashing these kids… I can live with it on one hand."

"But on the other hand you'd still arrest me."

He shrugged and went back to watching the game.

I wanted to spill my guts. I wanted to tell Keane everything I'd done over the years, and how it wasn't technically a bad thing. But I knew who he was and he was starting to figure out who I was, and this still wasn't going to end well. I wasn't going to be the big hero and turn myself in. Real life didn't work like that. If I confessed I wouldn't serve a few months in a cushy country club prison and then walk away like in every bad movie, off to live a quiet life with no regrets and looking like the good guy.

Real life was hard prison, where I'd be tortured and worse when every millionaire, celebrity and drug lord figured out I took their money without taking out their trash. I'd be dead inside of a week, and the bad guys would fight over who got to make the call for someone to shank me.

Reggie would turn me in because it was the lawful thing to do, and he obeyed the rules. He'd put aside his own personal beliefs because he was paid to follow the letter of the law, and the only way this worked for him would be if I went to prison.

"I don't suppose you want to talk off the record?" Reggie asked.

"I don't think you could. You're the super cop who is always on duty, Reggie. If there was something to confess, do you think I'd really do it? At a baseball game? Please don't tell me you're wearing a wire or your phone has the stupid app on it," I said and held my half-empty beer in the air. He knew the implication: I'd destroy the damn phone if I had to.

Reggie laughed. "No. This is a semi-social visit. I don't play games. If I want to talk to you I'll drag you down to an interrogation room and hold you for a few hours like I always do. I'm done with the game, though. I'm done playing dumb around you and hoping to catch you in a lie. You're too good at what you do."

"I sell baseball cards to people who want baseball cards," I said.

"You keep sticking to your story. I'm fine with it, because when I catch you red-handed it will make this sweeter," Reggie said.

"Your tone changed. You seem meaner, and I don't like it. I thought we were enjoying a night out. Just us guys. Why are we always talking shop? Frankly, I was having fun hanging out with you, Reggie," I said.

"I'm having fun, too. Which is what makes all of this harder, you know? I actually like you. I've been chasing down men like Chenzo for years and when I look them in the face I see nothing but hatred and evil. I don't see it with you, though. With you... I see something more. I know you think whatever it is you're doing is the right way to do it, but I'm here to tell you to stop. Walk away. Sell your baseball cards and keep making more money than you could possibly spend." Reggie smiled and looked at my wardrobe. "And, for God's sake, start dating a woman with some fashion sense. You dress like you're still in high school."

FIVE

"Why didn't you just tell Keane what was going on? It isn't like you don't already have a few FBI guys in your pocket," Marisa said on the phone. I was standing in the rain, trying in vain to hail a cab outside JFK Airport.

"It isn't that simple and you know it. Keane isn't going to just pat me on the back and let me know I'm doing a wonderful job and offer to buy me another beer. He'll toss me in prison in a heartbeat." Marisa just didn't get it. I was getting irritated and soaking wet. "Why didn't you get me a car again?"

"You told me not to. Twice. Even though I told you the weather was going to be bad in New York. You act like you're poor and it's annoying," Marisa said.

"I'm having no luck with a ride." I went back inside the terminal to dry off, or at least stop from getting wet.

"I have one on standby. He'll be there in fifteen minutes. You owe me," Marisa said.

I owed her for many, many times she'd bailed me out of messes, small ones like this and much larger ones. "Thanks. I appreciate it."

"When we hang up you need to pull the battery and chip from the phone and drop all the pieces in different garbage cans. Can you handle it?"

"Of course." I'd stopped asking her the why of certain things. I had so many of these burner phones and when Marisa deemed it time to destroy another one I went with the program. If there was even a hint we'd been hacked or someone was listening she wanted the phone gone. She'd done something to each of them to make it harder to listen to our conversations and to hack them, but I'd stared at her blankly when she tried to explain it once. Now, she just told me what to do.

And I happily did it.

By the time I'd gotten rid of the phone parts a car had pulled up and I was on my way to Manhattan. I was still wet but didn't want to waste time going to the hotel and getting changed first. I knew once I was in for the night I wasn't going back out. It would be room service and finding a game on the television for me.

I had three addresses for Will (or Little Chenzo?) I needed to check out, all in a bad area of the Bowery. I didn't expect the guy to be hanging out in the nicer spots, but with the rain and only a couple of hours until darkness, I instructed the driver to cruise past the three addresses so I could get a feel for them. At night the streets would be alive with people coming and going, hustling and making a not-so-honest living.

I knew I was wasting time. It wasn't like I was going to cruise by the right address and someone would come running out of the building, dramatically in the rain, and hand me a clue before disappearing into the night.

I didn't want to spend another night in a hotel by myself.

I wasn't the kind of guy to go find a street walker or call an escort service or hang out in sleazy bars and try to find someone drunk and easy. I also didn't want to find something long-term, but sometimes a friend to share a couple of drinks with and a laugh wasn't so bad. I traveled too much and with so many homes spread out across the U.S. I never had time to get real roots into any one area.

The sports card community was excellent and I had plenty of people in the business and as customers I could have a great time with at a show, but there were no social calls. I spent my life watching a ballgame or reading a book on my Kindle about sports. What a life.

"Are you familiar with New York City?" I asked the driver as we slowed in front of the first stop, a dilapidated two-story with boarded up windows. It looked like every other building on the block. If Will had spent time inside it was sucking on a crack pipe.

"What are you looking for?" the driver asked and I could almost see the smile. I'm sure he catered to rich, married men who got off a plane, called an expensive car service like this and part of the high cost was the fact the driver knew where to go no matter what you were looking for and could keep his mouth shut no matter what.

"I need a drink."

He shrugged in the driver's seat. "I could name fifty bars within a square mile. What exactly are you looking for, or does it matter? This isn't really a good neighborhood."

"I need someplace decent. Not too fancy but not a dump," I said.

He was driving again and glanced in the rearview mirror at me. "Do you have clothes you want to change into? You're still wet and very casual."

I laughed. Jean shorts, a black t-shirt and a pair of black Converse All-Star high-tops were my normal wear. I knew I probably looked like an old guy trying to act like a young guy. Marisa had finally convinced me wearing my Braves cap backwards wasn't a good look for me, either.

"I need to change first," I said.

"I know a spot not too far, once we get out of the area. You can change or buy a new set of threads. Up to you," the driver said.

"Sounds like a plan." It really didn't. Already I was wishing I'd asked to get me to the hotel so I could get changed into my sleep pants and another black t-shirt and watch TV.

I wasn't surprised when we pulled into a parking garage and I was led by the driver to an elevator. Even when things were legal (or seemed legit) people loved the air of secrecy and the games.

"Go to floor seven. Jacques is expecting you. Take your time," my driver said.

I handed him a fifty dollar bill and he gave a polite nod. Now it made me wonder if I'd under-tipped the guy or maybe he was expecting a twenty. No tip? I hated all these non-rule rules in life. The amount wasn't the issue. It's knowing what the *right* amount for things like this was.

Jacques was, indeed, expecting me, and he offered me a glass of wine and a quick tour of his suite. It wasn't a storefront, although they usually never are. A designer would rather entertain you in a private setting, away from the glare of customers and employees. Jacques wanted to not only sell me something expensive but keep selling me expensive something's over and over, each time I landed in New York.

It was a simple setup like I'd seen in big cities: small, cramped rooms with a large open studio area faced with giant windows. I knew the rent was astronomical and unnecessary unless you wanted to brag you could afford it, or give the allusion you could.

"Are you in town often?" Jacques asked as he took my measurements.

"Often enough." I decided to be vague. I was in a mood after being soaked and not being able to make a decision when it came to how I spent my night. I was also paranoid after Keane's bold but otherwise sloppy move in Boston and Little Chenzo washing ashore and the multitude of problems it caused me. Across the river, on the Jersey side, was Chenzo as well. I hated being this close to danger but I really had no choice.

"Is there a particular style you're looking for? A certain cut?" Jacques was staring at me, his wine glass tipped at an odd angle for effect. He was doing everything he could to get me to loosen up and spend too much money. A true salesman.

We chatted about the crummy weather and traffic in Manhattan and anything else he wanted to talk about, all the while trying to casually up-sell me on a string of suits I would rarely wear.

"I'm really looking for something to wear tonight," I said. "If I like it I'll order a few for home."

"Where is home?"

I always hesitate when asked this simple question. "Atlanta."

"You don't have a southern accent. If I had to guess I'd say Midwest," Jacques said. He, of course, had a thick French accent I was positive was faked. He was probably a failed actor, originally from Los Angeles by way of Boise, and had stumbled into expensive clothing on the opposite coast after never making it in movies or TV.

"I travel extensively across the country and sometimes the world," I said.

"I read somewhere your accent is set on the schoolyard as a child. I'm not sure I believe it. What line of work are you in, if you don't mind me asking?"

"Sports cards and memorabilia," I said. I looked out the enormous windows of the flat and could see the pelting rain against the glass, tinkling sounds as it struck. As a kid I loved the comforting sound of a heavy rainfall.

Jacques disappeared behind a set of screens in the room.

My new phone, the one I'd unwrapped as soon as I'd destroyed the last one, rang. I knew it was Marisa since no one else had the number.

"When do you want to go to Montreal?" she asked.

"A couple of days. Maybe three. I'll dig around here tomorrow but then I'd like to sleep in my own bed for a change," I said.

"Which bed?"

It was a legitimate question. "The flat in Pawtucket. I can rent a car and drive it."

"I'll get you a car," Marisa said.

I sighed. I know she loves helping me and I'm scatterbrained most of the time, but I needed a few hours to escape. Once in awhile I liked to be off the grid in a car, listening to bad radio and stopping at greasy spoon diners along the way.

"I'm fine," I said.

To her credit Marisa didn't push it any further. I guess she could tell I was having a moment and needed some space. I told you I didn't have it all together all the time, only when it was really needed.

"You got it, Boss. Call me in the morning if you change your mind," Marisa said and disconnected. I knew she was annoyed with me, and it wasn't just my insistence at driving myself. The Caruso incident was nagging at her as well, since she'd done so much to never let me get near to a client again. Yet, I was always walking into the hornet's nest and trouble. I wondered if I had a death wish or just wanted to sabotage my life at times.

"Is everything alright, sir?" Jacques asked as he stepped out with a gorgeously handsome black pinstripe suit.

I smiled and waved him off without an answer. I wanted to remain vague and I was getting tired, wondering what I was doing here again.

The suit felt like a second skin and I didn't bother to ask what the price was because then I'd balk even though I could afford it and many more.

"I'll take it. Do you have it in any other colors?" I asked.

"Of course. I got lucky on this fitting but I need to take it in right here and there," Jacques said, running his fingers lightly over the suit.

"Don't bother. I'll take it as-is. I like the feel of it. I'll need another black with pinstripes, two black without, and three dark suits your choice. I'll have my secretary contact you in the morning," I said, knowing Marisa would be pissed if she knew I called her my secretary. Even though she did everything one would do, she preferred personal assistant. Six of one, half a dozen of the other.

"Excellent." Jacques handed me his card. I knew better than to hand him a credit card. Deals like this were done by the secretaries... I mean personal assistants. We couldn't be bothered with the arduous task of swiping credit cards.

I would never understand what having money meant to most people, and I'd stumbled into it at an early age. Some would say I didn't appreciate it, and maybe they were right. On a slow night about a year ago, while watching a repeat on the Investigation Discovery Channel, I did the mental math about how much I'd need to spend a day in order to spend every dime I had to that point. I don't remember the exact number but I know it was ridiculous. Skimming the interest from all these accounts wasn't fast enough. I'd since grown bored with buying homes and cars. Some days I wish I had a bad cocaine problem or drank too much, because I was restless.

I decided (I swore to myself for the hundredth time) I'd make an effort to date someone. Anyone. A first date wasn't going to kill me, and I needed to hang around with someone who wasn't rich or was tied up somehow in what I did, either legal or illegal.

Jacques was staring at me again. He'd been asking me questions and I was off daydreaming.

"Is there anything else, sir?"

I shook my head, plastered a smile on my face, tried not to worry about my cheeks flushed with embarrassment and headed for the door.

In the elevator I checked out the suit in the mirrored doors and smiled. I looked good. I also looked tired. I had bags under my eyes and my skin looked grayish. I looked fat and looked much older than I was.

"Stop acting like a diva," I whispered. If a dude was with me right now he'd pull my Man Card. I wouldn't be able to argue, either.

The doors to the elevator opened and I jumped back, ready to strike.

It was my driver and he was smiling.

"You alright?" he asked, trying not to laugh.

"What are you doing? You almost got punched in the face and knocked out," I said.

He didn't look like he believed me. Right now I didn't believe me. I'd lost a step or three. Ten-fifteen years ago I would've broken his neck without hesitation and then tried to figure out where to dump the body. I was hoping I hadn't pissed my pants.

I needed a vacation.

"We have a slight bump in the road," the driver said.

He led me to the car and pushed the key fob, opening the trunk.

There was a man's body inside with a bashed-in skull. I didn't recognize the poor bastard.

"Friend of yours?" the driver asked.

I shook my head. I wasn't much of a fighter unless I was cornered, although I could hold my own. It wasn't as if I was bad at it, just I didn't like doing it. Physical confrontation was not my thing unless it was last resort.

"He tried to sneak up and put a bullet in my head, but I'd been watching since you got in the elevator. There was another guy in a black sedan but he took off when I beat his partner with his own pistol."

"How big was the pistol?" I asked. The damage was extensive. My driver was a big man but it would take half an hour to break a skull this bad. I hoped it wasn't what he'd been doing while I was getting fitted for a suit.

"I dragged him to the trunk and used the tire iron."

"That makes sense," I said. I looked at the driver for signs I was next or he'd ask some questions. Instead, he closed the trunk and opened my door.

"Your suit looks nice. Are you still up for a bar?" he asked.

I waited until he got into the driver's seat to answer. "No. I think I've had enough excitement for the night. Just drop me off at the hotel."

He nodded and started the car.

"Should I ask what happens next?" This wasn't the first time I'd been in a car with a body in the trunk, but it still freaks me out.

"Your personal assistant took care of the details. I'll drop you off and wait on the next block for an hour in case we were followed. A man named Robert will meet you in the lobby in the morning and make sure you get out of New York City in one piece."

"I need to check out the three locations first," I said.

The driver shrugged. "I'll let Robert know. He can drive you."

I realized I didn't know the driver's name, and I thought it was a good thing.

SIX

Unlike sitcoms and hour-long dramatic television, life rarely lets you solve one mystery before the next one comes along, right as the previous one is tied up with a pretty bow and put away.

I was still dealing with the Little Chenzo stuff when Marisa called, and it had taken another turn for the worst last night after meeting Jacques. Not to mention the dead guy in the trunk. I decided not to ask Marisa about any of it, because I really didn't want to know too much. I was starting to realize how good she was.

"Boss, we got another job. This one is a bad one, too. Older subject in Las Vegas," she said.

I hated trying to subdue an older kid. Babies were easy. You snuck in, tried to keep them from crying, and stepped out. With older kids you sometimes had a fight if you didn't do it quickly, and there were also the problems that came with a subject who knew who his family, friends, life, etc. had been and didn't understand what was happening.

Those kids had to be more or less brainwashed into believing they were someone else. I had a doctor somewhere in Dallas who specialized in this part of the journey, but I didn't know a thing about him. It might even be a *her* for all I knew. The system was in place a long time before I got here, and it would evolve as we progressed. Marisa had made vast improvements in the network over the years, too.

"She's just turned fifteen. High school student. She's a cheerleader. Stays after school for practice and walks home. Three blocks. Easy," Marisa said.

Marisa liked to downplay how hard this was, as if I've ever complained or said I couldn't do a job. I'd take the money and do this because I could only imagine what the alternative would be. I guess a legitimately dead kid somewhere.

"What timeframe are we talking?" I asked. I could feel a headache coming on.

The ride from Manhattan to Pawtucket had been wonderful. I'd figured out how to use the satellite radio and found a decent hard rock station, singing along to Led Zeppelin and Motley Crue. Sue me. I'm old.

"Within the week. Obviously Monday through Friday so she'll be in school and you can get her. Tell me what you need," Marisa said. She liked to play this game whenever we got a new job. And it wasn't just me. It was a *we* when it came to making these successful.

I'd been in Marisa's shoes for a few years until my boss had retired and handed me the reins to this business. It had been in the eighties and I had to scramble to do everything the old fashioned way: putting dimes in a payphone booth. For the younger generation feel free to Google it and see how they used to work.

I was formulating a plan in my head. "I'll need a beat-up white van. A work van. A good disguise and something to render her unconscious in seconds before she screams," I said. I wanted to create the perfect illusion of a pedophile grabbing a pretty teen girl off the street and getting her into his van. I'd need an escape route and a safe place to switch her into another car and away before the cops showed up.

"I'll need to talk to the father or whoever is paying me."

"No way. We've been over this before. Look what happened in Philly. Don't you get it? There is absolutely no good reason to meet anyone, and they don't want to meet you. They just want to wire the money to an account and act surprised when their little princess is abducted," Marisa said.

She was right, but it still felt odd to not see this horrible person eye to eye.

An older teen was also a gray area for me, as there was obviously no way to simply hand the kid over to a new set of parents to raise as their own with no questions asked. I'd need to put this girl away for awhile until I could figure out what to do with her, and killing wasn't an option.

The easy part was the kidnapping. Getting her unconscious into the van and speeding away was exciting, and the adrenaline rush was going to keep me wired and going until I got to the safe house.

When she woke up, though, would be where the hard part began. I couldn't just keep her on ice indefinitely. I could waste my time trying to convince her she was safe now, but there was no chance in hell she'd believe her kidnapper. If I told her what had really happened she'd think I was lying. I'd think I was lying if I were in her shoes. Her shoes probably cost more than my entire wardrobe, and I owned two dozen pair of jean shorts and more black t-shirts than was sane.

I tried to remember the last time I'd had to do this with an older subject.

"Boss. You still there?" Marisa asked over the phone.

"Huh? Yeah. Just daydreaming again. I'm trying to recall the last teenager job."

"It was July of 2005. Harry something or other. Remember? He was fifteen. You did the job in Portland," Marisa said.

"Portland? Yeah, I remember. It was cold in Maine, right?"

"Who knows? You grabbed Harry in Portland *Oregon*. You really should see a doctor about your memory loss. I worry about you," Marisa said.

"I'm playing with you," I lied. "Didn't he end up in foster care? He got sent to the weird doctor in Dallas to brainwash him or something." I'd never met the doc in Texas but he seemed really creepy over the phone. He also charged a huge amount of cash but he got results. "I think I'm going to need to get to Dallas with the girl, too."

"I'll start working on a car and places to stay. That's a long trip from Vegas with an unwilling passenger. You might need to keep her sedated," Marisa said. "I figure nineteen hours if you don't have to stop much."

There was always a chance something could go really cross-eyes if you kept someone out for too long, and I didn't want the worry. I had no real idea how else I'd survive such a long car ride, though. Maybe a stop at a sleazy hotel would work to break up the drive. A dude carrying an unconscious teen into a hotel room wouldn't warrant a second glance at some places. Marisa needed to find one halfway to Dallas.

"How are we looking for my Montreal trip?" I asked.

"You're booked and all set. I e-mailed you everything you need and downloaded the ticket to the other phone," Marisa said.

"Which phone?"

"The two blue stripes, old man," Marisa said. We went through so many numbers and phones I sometimes needed help figuring out which one I was using. When carrying a cell phone became the norm and I no longer needed my beeper, I'd often taken the wrong burner with me or the active phone in my suitcase would ring while the one in my pocket wasn't even working.

Marisa solved it by adding markings on each phone and synchronizing us so we knew which phone was in operation. Really, it was for me.

"I'll spend two days in Montreal unless there's trouble. Then I'll head to Las Vegas and take care of this job. I need to stay focused and not lose any ground with the Little Chenzo thing," I said.

"Will Black. Don't call him Little Chenzo. His father gave up the right when he had him killed, remember?" Marisa took this serious. Sometimes more serious than I did. I guess her wounds of abandonment were still fresher than mine, and I'd long ago made peace with it.

I also knew who the bastards were who tried to have me killed. One of the perks of taking over for your predecessor. I supposed the first thing Marisa would do when or if I turned this all over to her was to find out who her real parents were.

That's exactly what I did, and I regretted doing it every day since. But I could talk to her for hours about not doing it (like had happened to me) and I knew she'd look. And forever hate the fact she did.

"What are Will's parent's names again?" I asked.

"Frank and Delores Black."

"Frank Black? Like the guy from The Pixies?"

"Who?"

I groaned. "Forget it." Damn kids don't appreciate good music anymore. They want pretty people singing inane lyrics to a simple dance beat while gyrating across a stage.

Damn kids, get off my lawn.

Yeah, I'm an old man.

"I'll send over as much intel as I can collect tonight. At the hotel you'll be receiving a package and in the box is a laptop with everything downloaded. I'll walk you through it so you can turn it on," Marisa said.

"Not funny."

"I thought it was," Marisa said. "You have your passport already."

"Yes, ma'am. Larry Jones. I like it. Can I ask people to call me Chipper?"

"Don't get cute. This is one of the reasons Keane is sniffing around so closely now. You need to stop being so cocky and get the job done," Marisa said.

I felt reprimanded but I deserved it. I had been too cocky lately.

"On the laptop you'll also find a few outstanding sports card orders and bills I need you to look over. If you want me to pay them just let me know. You also have a query about a few Atlanta Braves cards," Marisa said.

"You already know the answer is no to selling my personal collection."

"They're looking for bulk commons from the 1990's. Offering a penny apiece, which is way more than they're worth."

"They're worth more to me. Tell the client thanks but no thanks. I'm not selling anything Braves. We've had this discussion too many times," I said.

"Fine. I don't get it but you're the boss."

"Yes, I am."

"Your driver is waiting downstairs, by the way," Marisa said.

"I don't need him. Pay them for the time but tell them to go away."

"Obviously I heard about last night. It's a new driver and they'll be taking more precautions," Marisa said.

"Someone supposedly wanted to kill me. Why do you think that is? How did they know I was here? I have too many unanswered questions to put my life into anyone's hands right now. I'm not climbing into the backseat of a car with tinted windows and getting shot," I said.

"Did you watch *Goodfellas* again?"

"No."

"Are you sure?"

I sighed. "It was on last Saturday but I only watched the last hour. Ninety minutes tops. It has nothing to do with my paranoia. You know what does? A dead guy in a trunk who supposedly wanted me dead."

"Why do you keep saying supposedly?"

"I'm not sure. Practicing for a future court appearance, I guess. Regardless, I'll take a cab. At least I'll know if I die it won't be from an assassin. It will be from the smell and bad driving," I said.

* * * * *

This address couldn't be right. I turned back to the cab driver and motioned for him to roll down the window, asking if this was the address I gave him.

He shrugged and double-checked his GPS against the address I'd given him, finally giving me the thumbs up without another word. He rolled the window back up and I looked at the closed jazz club in front of me.

I guess I was expecting another crack house like all the others I'd attempted to visit today. No one knew Will Black so far, but ninety-nine percent of the people I'd talked to had no idea what their own name was at the moment.

When I knocked on the door I wasn't surprised to wait and find no one nice enough to answer it. I checked my phone for the time.

I remember the old days when I wore a watch or else I'd have no idea what time it was. Sure, restaurants and banks and businesses might have a clock in view for the customers but just walking down the street? You needed a nice watch. I had seven or eight expensive Rolexes in my homes I never took out of the drawer anymore. I wasn't the kind of guy to flash the jewelry and it only invited thugs in places like this.

The club itself was smashed between two other buildings and I'd have to walk all the way around a city block to see if there was a back door or parking lot. Frankly, I was tired and lazy at this point. I wasn't going to find out anything, anyway. Marisa had mentioned Will was a musician and I guessed he was allowed to flop in this joint around gigs.

I took a few steps towards the cab when I got an eerie feeling. I turned quickly and scanned the building, and sure enough, someone was watching me from a third floor window.

It was a brief glimpse of someone with long, stringy hair and missing their teeth. Maybe a guy in his thirties? It was hard to say.

I renewed my quest to get inside, banging on the door over and over until my hand hurt.

"I know you're home. Open the door. I'm not the cops. I'm looking for a friend," I yelled.

When I stepped back and looked up a thin curtain moved but the toothless guy didn't appear again. I didn't know what to do.

Kicking in the door to a club was only going to get me arrested, and I had too much to do this week. Marisa bailing me out of jail wouldn't be too hard but it would set me back and put my face back on Keane's radar. He'd also figure out another alias of mine if I wasn't careful.

Standing on the sidewalk, staring at the building, wasn't helping. It wasn't getting me inside, either. I could forget my Montreal plans and stick around until tonight when the club might be open, but then it would set my next job back and I didn't know how much time I had.

I got back into the cab and told the driver to take me back to my hotel. I'd be back in a few days to deal with this wrinkle in my plans.

SEVEN

I had the distinct feeling this Montreal visit was going to be a bust. I knew from my Canadian resources the FBI had already paid a visit to Little Chenzo's parents home. I knew it was Keane and he knew what I knew, but I wondered if now the world knew.

Had the parents already rolled over and told the FBI they'd illegally adopted the kid all those years ago? If they'd kept anything other than the bogus paperwork it could eventually get traced right back to me.

I also needed to get back to New York so I could get into the club and ask a few questions before an overlarge bouncer tossed me out into the alley.

An older man with white hair greeted me at the door with squinty eyes. He held the door open a crack and didn't say a word.

"Mister Black?"

After way too long he nodded but remained silent.

"I'm with the government," I said. I liked to be as vague as possible until they asked some questions. Then I could take out one of the fake badges I had hidden in my jacket.

He continued to stare without a sound.

"Do you speak English?" I asked.

He understood because he looked annoyed. "What do you want? You aren't from my government. You Americans have no jurisdiction in Canada, yet you keep coming to my door."

"I'm really sorry for bothering you. I just have a couple of follow-up questions to ask about your son, Will," I said, trying to sound official and solemn and try to get the guy to relax.

It wasn't working.

"I have nothing more to say," Mister Black said. "Good day."

He had a thick French Canadian accent and I wondered if Will had had one before he died. I'm not sure why it even mattered, but knowing he was born into a Jersey Italian family made it seem surreal.

"If I can just come in and ask a few simple questions. Please," I said.

"Like I told the FBI agent yesterday, until you find my son I'm not interested in talking to anyone else," he said.

Had Keane been here already? Gotten ahead of me? Damn. I was doing too much and this should've been my priority. While I was wasting time in New York City he had caught the first flight out of Boston and headed to Canada. I know it was Keane. Actually, at this point, I hoped it was. If it was someone associated with Chenzo we were all in trouble.

More than likely, Keane had spilled the beans about their dead son but I figured I'd give it a shot myself and see what I could shake out of the tree.

"I have some bad news," I said. I dipped my head slightly. He hadn't shut the door yet, which I took to be a good sign. I needed to spring this on him so he'd drop his guard and let me in. I had a vision of his wife crying on the couch while Frank comforted her and I could slowly pry as much info as possible from the elder couple.

"What news now?" Frank asked.

"I'm afraid your son, Will, washed up on a Massachusetts beach a couple of days ago."

He didn't look shocked and he didn't cry, or scream or do much of anything other than stare at me. I figured Keane had told them the news but maybe he didn't give them all of the details and I was going to string it along as far as I could at this point.

"Unless you finally did find Will, I think you are mistaken," he said.

"We did. He washed up," I said.

Frank shook his head and smirked. "You're as stupid as the American police officers who called us yesterday. My wife flew down to Boston to claim his body. Guess what? It wasn't him. Not our son, although I wouldn't have been surprised if it was the way he lives his life."

Now it was my turn to be in shock. "There's been a mistake."

"No mistake on our part. My wife is on her way home now. No one is going to reimburse us for the money we had to pay for a short flight, either. I have a right mind to sue everyone. You understand what I'm saying? Hundreds it cost for the ticket and hotel and food," Frank said.

I took out my wallet and slipped five hundred dollar bills from it, holding them up.

Frank's eyes got wide.

"Let me in. Give me fifteen minutes of your time. I really need to ask you some questions. Please," I said.

Frank stepped aside and I could see the wheels turning in his head. I'm not a cynical man, but everyone had their price. I sometimes wondered in times like this if I could've gotten my foot in the door with a crisp fifty. I had no time to waste, though. Usually on jobs I could spread it out, enjoy the planning and look at it from all angles.

This wasn't a job. This was covering up a job that got away from me from my past. I wondered how many others would someday bite me.

Before I could sit on his worn couch I was talking, taking in the dull furniture and fading pictures on the walls.

"I thought I heard you say it wasn't Will," I said.

"William," Frank said defensively. He was jittery, his hands moving in his lap.

I put up a hand. "I'm not the cops. Not the FBI."

Frank started to rise from his chair. "Then get out of my house."

"I was the man who got you Will when he was just a baby," I said. I knew I was breaking my own rules but I felt the press of time on my shoulders right now. Dancing around the issue and hoping this guy understood was not an option today. Too much at stake, like my life and livelihood.

"I don't understand. We adopted from Saint Mark's."

I shook my head. "I'm going to tell you something that can never be repeated, even to your wife. This information is so sensitive because it is dangerous. I need you to nod your head and tell me you get it," I said. I was playing a dangerous game and I knew it.

Frank nodded his head.

"Your son was part of a Mob hit. A very important person. High-ranking mobster. But he wasn't killed, obviously. He was rescued and hidden away. Given to a nice family in Montreal named Black. Never told where he came from or who he really was. Only… maybe the bad guys have figured out who he was. When the body washed ashore I thought it was Will. William. But now you're telling me it wasn't him?"

Frank nodded. I could see the old man was on the verge of tears. His hands had stopped moving.

"My wife verified it wasn't William. Not our son, although she said it looked like him. Whoever it was even had his old Army jacket on with the pins," Frank said.

"It was definitely his jacket?"

"Yes. She noticed the rip on the sleeve and he had all these patches sewn onto it and pins from these horribly named musical groups he liked, even as a small child." Frank put his head down. "He was so angry, even before his teen angst years. So physically violent."

"You sent him away?" I asked gently.

Frank's head snapped up and there was anger in his eyes. "We threw him out. At twelve. Tossed him into the street like garbage. We never got help for William. We just gave up on the boy."

I stared at Frank because I had no follow-up question or comment. I was trying to process this information and see if it was relevant to anything. When Marisa had told me they abandoned the kid I thought she was cutting to the chase. I assumed counseling and individual therapy, maybe family counseling, had been done. All avenues exhausted. Will ran away at twelve and his parents wept for the boy each and every night.

The Black family had let a child walk away, one they'd sworn to protect. They'd adopted the kid from what was usually a bad situation. Foster care. The system. Birth parents who didn't want them. Abandonment issues.

I wanted to punch this old man in the face.

"That was it?" I asked.

Frank nodded and reached under the chair cushion, pulling out a flask. He offered me a sip but I declined. He took such a large pull I figured half of the flask was now empty.

"Did you see Will in the last few years?"

Frank wiped his mouth and smacked his lips. He was a drunk and an alcoholic. Maybe Will getting away from this guy was a good thing, although based on the stories I'd heard so far about Will's life, it was six of one and half a dozen of the other. I liked that expression.

"My wife ran into him at the Port Authority once, about two years ago. She was on her way to meet her sister for lunch. She said he looked like death warmed over. Slumped against the wall with nothing but a sleeping bag filled with junk. A tin can for tips. He was playing his guitar for change. Probably for drugs and alcohol," Frank said.

I declined pointing at the flask in his hand and let him continue.

"When he saw my wife, you know what he did?" Frank asked.

I wanted to say spit on her but I just stared.

"He spit on her. Can you believe it?"

I stood. "Yes. I can. You and your wife threw out a kid who'd already been thrown out. You abandoned a twelve year old little boy with anger issues. Instead of getting Will help you... you're a horrible person, and so is your damn wife." I was livid and my hands were shaking in anger.

I wasn't a violent man, per se, but this guy was pushing all the right buttons. In case you hadn't already guessed, I took protecting children very seriously. My job was to take them from an abysmal situation and put them with loving, caring people. I did this at great risk. Sure, the money was amazing but I'd do it for free if I knew it would help a kid.

The Black family had taken damaged goods and further crushed it. William Black had been dealt the worst hand ever, and I felt sorry for the kid. What chance did he have? I know the bleeding heart Liberals will moan about how bad this kid had it, and for once I agreed.

"Get out of my house," Frank said and tried to stand.

I moved two steps forward and chopped him in the throat without a thought. I'm not a violent person, I told myself as I cocked my fist back.

"I'm going to ask you a few more questions and then I'll leave. You'll answer them truthfully and the five hundred is yours. I'll add another hundred to keep your mouth shut. Got it? I wasn't here. Do we have a deal?" I kept my fist ready to strike. I was actually hoping he'd say something stupid or curse at me so I could unload and beat him to within an inch of his life.

I'm really not a violent person, but I can be pushed like anyone else.

Frank sat down and finished off what little was left in his flask, rubbing his throat.

"Do you have anything left of his?"

Frank shook his head.

"Why didn't you tell anyone you got rid of him like a sack of garbage?"

Frank sighed. When he spoke his voice cracked and he was in obvious pain from the throat chop, which made me happy.

"We were still collecting from the state. We needed the money but not the problem," Frank said.

"You sicken me," I said. I knew it was cliché but it fit.

Frank glared. "William tried to set the house on fire during one of his meth binges. He built a lab in the garage at ten. At ten. The kid was a menace and couldn't be controlled. He was glad to leave and so were we."

I had serious doubts the kid had built a meth lab. I'm sure he smoked pot and maybe did some hard stuff but cooking his own? No way. Frank was making excuses and trying to paint himself as the victim.

"What else can you tell me about him? If it wasn't Will on the beach, where could he be?"

Frank shrugged. "Check Port Authority or the sewers. You can't miss the dirty bum. He looked like a rat with his gray skin and missing all his teeth from the drugs."

Missing all his teeth.

The toothless guy in the upstairs window of the jazz club was Will Black.

Alive and well. For now.

EIGHT

The white van smelled like bleach and I had to roll the windows down so I didn't choke on the fumes. Whoever Marisa got the van from was new at this, because a clean vehicle just meant no fingerprints or receipts to McDonalds under the seat. Not a new clean and polish. I needed this to look old and grungy, like a real work van. The cops needed to be out looking at the million plumbers, carpenters, flooring guys and whoever else drove these things so I could get away.

Instead, I was in the shiniest white van in Las Vegas. I was sparkling down the road, an eyesore for drivers around me. If I hadn't already set everything into motion and needed to drive out and to Texas as soon as possible I would've called Marisa and had her find a new van and fire whoever she was working with on this bright thing.

I usually drove past the location three or four times when I wanted to be seen, but with the van so obviously new, most of the work vans in the city would be eliminated by the cops. As soon as I dumped it and switched cars I knew it would be a race to get as many miles away from Vegas before it was found.

Yeah, I know. I keep talking about it but lately things were bugging me more than usual. I really didn't need this job. Definitely not for the money, but for the sheer fact I was too busy to really get behind it. You needed to commit both mentally and physically, and I was still thinking about Will Black in the window.

I took a leisurely drive past the school, already let out and only a few cars in the parking lot. With any luck, the school cameras would pick up on the van and get the tag number, which was yanked from another car.

Damn, I hoped it was. Didn't everyone know that was how you did it? Based on the van I now had my doubts.

I called Marisa and complained about the situation.

"Stop whining and get it done," Marisa said. She had a way with words. Just for the record: when my voice swells a couple of octaves it isn't whining. It's getting excited. Big difference. "They stole a new van since they had short notice. The plates are jacked from another van, which will throw the cops for a second. Enough to get you out of Dodge."

"I'm in Vegas, not Dodge."

She didn't even bother to tell me how lame my joke was.

"How's the surveillance in New York going?" I asked.

She groaned loudly on the phone.

I was supposed to be working and when you were in the midst of a job you never worried about the previous one or the next one. But in all fairness, Will Black wasn't an upcoming job. He was a problem I needed to sort out before Keane or Chenzo figured out where he was hiding.

"I have a guy on it. Don't worry. The club was open last night and two of them went inside and listened to boringly smooth jazz for hours," Marisa said.

"What came of it?"

"They both hate jazz even more, I imagine. Will Black never made an appearance and they couldn't get up the stairs to the apartments. Too many eyes watching. There is definitely something going on in the building, but it could just be drug trafficking. According to what they heard, the joint is only open Friday night through Sunday afternoon," Marisa said.

"Did you call it a joint?"

Marisa laughed. "Just hip to the jazz lingo, mulligan."

"I think mulligan means cop, or something to do with golf?" I had no idea but I knew she had used it wrong. She needed to work on her jazz slang.

"Anyway… it's being looked at. Not any of your concern right now. You need to focus on the task at hand, see?" She said this in a really bad 1950's mobster movie voice, which made me laugh.

I hadn't laughed in awhile and it felt good.

"Are you wearing a disguise?" Marisa asked.

"Yes," I answered reluctantly. I never showed her what I had done to change my appearance but it never stopped her from asking.

"Take a selfie and send it to me."

"I don't know what a selfie is but I'm not sending one to you," I said. Part of the fun was her going out of her mind trying to guess what I was dressed like or what I'd done to my face for the job.

Five years ago I'd taken a newborn from a stripper in Kansas City. My disguise was an overweight blind woman who was in the neighborhood wandering around all day. When the stripper – I'll call her a woman so no one gets offended for whatever reason – walked by and into her apartment I followed. I was like a ghost. Just a poor blind soul out in the big, bad world.

I held the stripper, uh, woman up with a knife and took the kid.

The worst part of it? She barely put up a fight. I think she knew what the real deal was. Her small-time crook boyfriend was the baby daddy, and he paid a pretty penny to get rid of the kid before his wife found out.

Marisa, smiling, had told me three months later he was found dead in the back of the strip club he frequented. It seems he'd knocked up another stripper... ugh... woman, and this time her big-time crook husband took care of the guy.

Payback was a bitch, as they say.

The best part for me was the surveillance footage from the convenience store across the street. It clearly showed the blind woman entering the building behind the stripper and a few minutes later she didn't look all that blind, carrying a baby in her arms and walking quickly around the corner and out of sight.

Marisa loved it. Now, she asked a million questions after each job.

"I'm in position," I said as I parked the van down the street.

In case you were wondering, I was wearing my old man disguise I'd used before, mostly for California and the Pacific Northwest jobs over the years: a graying hair wig with matching moustache, thick Coke bottle glasses and a small red rose in my faded jacket pocket.

The rose was a nice touch and could tie this serial kidnapper into a few crimes and keep the FBI and local cops busy. You'd think putting them together would be bad for business, but I learned from my predecessor the best thing to do would be to give your fake evildoer some personality. Let the media run with it, and it would only hinder the investigations.

I was the Red Rose Kidnapper. Wanted in three States and I was about to add Nevada to the list. As long as I kept doing these jobs in this area of the country, no one would tie any of it into any of my other jobs.

The bogus tips would come pouring into the tip lines tonight, most of which would be whack jobs looking for their fifteen minutes of fame or the ones who believed an alien had taken over the children. The flood of bad tips would bury the one or two real ones until it was too late. I figured the FBI and local cops were still wading through the rivers of calls from years ago. I didn't have an ego so a letter mailed to the newspaper calling out law enforcement wasn't going to happen. All I wanted was to get this done and over with and move on so I could get back to the jazz club.

I saw the first cheerleader exiting the side gym door but it wasn't the target. She got into a waiting Hummer and drove off just as another two came out.

This wasn't like the high school I went to. It was clean and bright. The rich kids went here and these were the kids I despised growing up because I wanted to be them. I guess I am one of the rich kids now, just twice their age. Or more.

I glanced again at her picture on my phone. Heck, I could glance at four hundred of her pictures if I wanted to. Her Facebook page was wide open and her entire life, down to the fact she had sushi with her friend Dee two nights ago, she really thought one of the football players was hot, and she'd smoked more than a few joints since high school started.

I smiled, thinking of the word joint. I knew Marisa didn't have this experience in school. I'd watched her from a distance until she dropped out in ninth grade and started doing the wrong thing. Someday I was going to convince her to get her GED, but she didn't think it meant anything. Maybe she was right. She had enough street smarts for both of us combined, and I grew up in a rough neighborhood.

There she was. When I was doing a job I never used the target's name in my head. Too personal, even though I wasn't going to kill them. If I treated them like a human being I might hesitate, especially with an older kid. I'd clubbed a couple over the head in the past because they didn't cooperate and fought back. Which is the norm, but when you get a wired kid on drugs or someone who's been lifting weights since they were ten, it gets rough.

She was standing at the edge of the parking lot with two of her fellow cheerleaders, backpacks over their shoulders like a scene from *Beverly Hills: 90210*.

It was a show when I was this kid's age and it rocked. Look it up, it might be on Netflix.

The waiting was the hardest part. Any number of random occurrences could happen before I got to her: a nosy parent or teacher wondering what a pristine white van was doing in the school parking lot, a police cruiser on patrol because the extracurricular stuff was getting out at this time every day, or just bad luck. The only time I almost didn't finish a job was when the stolen car didn't start and I had to get a jump from what turned out to be a very friendly off-duty cop.

A car pulled up to the curb and her two friends got in, leaving her alone. She looked around, maybe trying to find someone else to talk to, but when she saw the rest of the cheerleaders were already gone she began the walk home.

I wondered why a kid this rich and high profile was hoofing it a few blocks. Didn't mom or dad want to protect her? Yeah, I know one of them was paying me an indecent amount of money to kill her, but you still needed the premise you loved your kid enough to get a car to pick her up.

I let her get almost out of sight before I started the van. No use trying to take her with a few cars still in the parking lot. Just ahead, around the first bend in the road, stood a vacant lot and the houses on either side were shielded with trees. The other side of the road had big houses set back. The perfect spot to do the job. I didn't need to be seen while doing it. I was sure the white van cruising the parking lot a couple of times and then leaving right after she did and heading in her direction would be enough to give the cops something to go on.

By the time they collected the camera tapes and talked to eyewitnesses I'd be long gone.

A woman sitting in her car, reading a book and waiting for her son or daughter, looked up and gave a half-smile. I waved and beamed with joy. She'd remember the old man with white hair and thick glasses, and by tomorrow night a police sketch would be on the local news channels.

The back of the van was ready to go, too. I had rope and a pile of moving rugs to cover her, as well as two pairs of handcuffs I had no intention of using unless she fought back. I'd be able to get the rag over her mouth before she knew what hit her, though, so I wasn't too worried about her resisting.

The first time I'd used a similar plan was a long time ago. I was taught by my predecessor. Who had been taught by his, I supposed. You never really talked about too much further back. Maybe the last generation of child abductors was enough. Maybe we all hoped the phone would stop ringing or the e-mails would never come, and the world would right itself and bad people would stop wanting their children dead.

I needed to hurry up and get back to New York.

She was just ahead now as I drove at about ten miles an hour, foot lightly tapping the gas to keep momentum. I'd get ahead of her and stop, acting like I was at the house for a reason. I was in a work van, and I was a heavy old man. No harm.

As I drove past I could see she was oblivious, wearing ear buds and listening to music I'm sure I didn't get or understand, deep in her high school thoughts.

She's a mark, I told myself. You never got too close and I needed to stop worrying about whom she was or what she was thinking about. I knew it was all the running around from city to city that was getting to me, and the change from east to west coast time always hit me hard. Especially as I got older.

I put the van in park but kept it running. With her music blasting she wouldn't know the difference anyway until it was too late.

Just as I opened the door I heard the gunshot.

The gun I was carrying was empty, here for effect in the event I needed it. Unconsciously I reached for it in my jacket pocket as if it would do me any good.

Who was shooting at me? Could it be one of Chenzo's boys? Payback for the guy in the trunk?

I looked around but didn't see anyone. I'd need to abort this job until I could figure out what had happened.

And then I figured it out with the second shot, which caught my target in the stomach. She was already on the ground, the first shot having ripped through her neck.

Someone had killed her.

I stomped on the gas and drove away, expecting a black sedan or a gunman to block my way out of the area.

Someone had really killed her.

NINE

"Calm down. Where are you?" Marisa was trying to get me to breathe and stop yelling but I couldn't. My heart was racing and I felt nauseous.

"They shot her. They shot her," I said. The reverse image of her in the side mirror as the second shot hit her lifeless body would be etched in my psyche forever.

"Pull yourself together. Where are you right now?"

"I'm in the van on the side of the road," I said.

"Are you crazy? Stick to the plan. Drive. Now."

I punched the steering wheel. "What plan? I don't have her because she's been shot. She was assassinated twenty feet from me."

"You need to get to the stashed car and drive towards Dallas. I'll figure it out on my end. If you stay in town you're going to get arrested for her murder. You set it up so the van and you were seen, remember? Whoever did this isn't going to be on any surveillance tapes," Marisa said.

"You're right. I'll call you back in an hour."

"I'll see what I can figure out. Hey… you gonna be alright?" Marisa asked.

I nodded my head even though Marisa couldn't see me as I started the van. "Yes, I'll be fine. This isn't the worst thing I've ever seen. Just not sure what happened."

"We're going to figure it out."

I hung up and drove a couple of miles over the speed limit, watching for police and ambulances, which both drove past me about a minute later. I was already a few miles away from the crime scene but I was paranoid not only the authorities but also the killer would get on my tail soon enough.

This had never happened to me. I couldn't remember ever hearing something like this going on. There was a code. You hired one person to do the job. It was very specific and I was sure Marisa had gone over it with the client.

A bad coincidence? The other parent wanted the girl dead, maybe? I hoped Marisa could make heads or tails out of what had happened.

I started to head south, my eyes darting from one mirror to the next. The ride to the new car was only ten minutes but it felt like ten hours, and I was expecting the window to shatter at any moment and my life to be over.

I cleaned out the van since it wouldn't make sense anymore. The new car was an old car, a Ford Taurus with Texas plates. I put the kidnapping kit in front seat with me and pulled off my wig and glasses. My eyes hurt from wearing them, even though the lenses themselves weren't anything more than plastic.

By the time I'd ditched the disguise in a gas station bathroom, gassed up the car and left parts of the kidnap kit in restaurant bathrooms along the way, Marisa was calling again.

"Are you ready for some messed up info?" she asked.

Sure. What did I have to lose at this point? "I'm all ears."

"You got paid for the job."

"I get paid half upfront and the rest when it's done. So?"

"I reverse-engineered this entire transaction. The money was paid the second I mentioned the dollar amount. The second. Before they'd even told me who the target was, and in full," Marisa said.

"That's uncommon but not suspicious." These jobs were from people who wanted this done once in their life, not multiple times. They were scared it was a police sting and even more scared they'd go to prison for a long time if it went south.

Sometimes they talked too much and they always paid on time or early, afraid I could use a late payment to squeeze them for more money. I never would but they didn't know any better. It was all part of the unwritten code but when you're dealing with people who want children dead, it gets into some gray areas.

"But get this… the guy who I talked to had nothing to do with the payment," Marisa said.

"Again, not uncommon. Is there a point to this? I need to find a hotel and crash and soak in a hot shower for a few hours," I said. I left out the part about more than likely crying myself to sleep. I needed a moment. I wasn't a cold blooded assassin, after all.

"I contacted the guy and he thanked me for a job well-done. He thinks you did it and praised his go-between for setting this up in the first place. The money went through his mysterious middle man. When I tried to follow the money trail further back it was a dead end. The company itself is part of another company, part of another company, and so forth," Marisa said.

All very common in this line of work. I had so many dummy companies and money hidden all over the world, if I needed to pull it all and run, I would miss half of it. The scary part was it was all mostly legal thanks to the corporate laws. I'll never get pinched for tax evasion or something stupid, because they'll never ever find this money. I pay enough taxes on the sports cards part of my life, anyway.

"I did find a name," Marisa said. "Nolan Ryan was the name given for the middle man."

"I'm guessing not the great pitcher. It's either a bad coincidence or someone knows what I'm doing with fake names. What chance is it Keane is involved? I never took him for a dirty cop," I said. I didn't believe in coincidences. Someone had taken great pains to screw up my job, still pay me for it, not take the credit, and call me out over the baseball naming I've been doing for years.

"If Keane is dirty I'll be amazed," Marisa said. She'd done her homework on the guy over the years. Besides his lousy marrying streak and driving, he was relatively clean. He drank a bit and cursed and never went to church, but he wasn't someone who could shoot down a sixteen year old girl in broad daylight.

"Maybe a rogue FBI agent. It could be anyone. I'm sure they'll get antsy when I don't try to find them right away," I said.

"Only because you need to cry in the shower for awhile."

"I never said anything about crying," I said defensively.

"It was definitely implied. Are you going to drive all the way to the hotel or do you want me to find you another one?"

"Find me something a couple of hours south but close to an airport if possible," I said.

"Tall order but I'll try. I'll keep everything booked at the hotel and airport from Texas in case someone is watching," Marisa said. I'd trained her to be as paranoid as I was at times. You could never be too careful and money was never the issue. Being cheap over canceling a flight early to save $400 was what got a guy caught in my book.

Before hanging up with Marisa I went through my little black book of killers I'd known over the years. "Any clue who it could be? Who is bold enough to do this?"

"Jesus Diaz comes to mind but no way that he killed a sixteen year old as sloppy as that," Marisa said.

"No. Diaz is working in Hollywood last I heard. We're not exactly friends but we don't do the same work, either."

Jesus was a good guy as far as hired killers go. I'd run into him a couple of years ago in New York. It was a brief meeting and we both had our fingers on the trigger. You never took it easy with another assassin, especially since I was just playing one. I wondered if Diaz was being a heavy for a movie guy or if he was actually acting. Maybe I'd look him up after my shower crying. I knew it wasn't him, but there were another dozen names I still needed to cross off my list. This week was getting worse and worse.

"I need to think for awhile. Do your thing and I'll text you when I get to the new hotel," I said.

"I just booked the hotel. I'll text the address and info right now," Marisa said.

I could never multi-task like she could, and if I tried this would all come crashing down around me. Even more than it seemed to be right now.

The long, winding road was welcome right now. I set the GPS on my phone with the hotel address. I had about ninety minutes until I reached my destination, which was plenty of time to sort out everything in my head. Maybe I'd have a good cry while I drove.

I knew I was missing something important in all of this. There was always something obvious. An old buddy of mine, Chet, used to smoke weed. A lot. In my teens I was doing some really stupid things including breaking and entering with Chet so we could afford pot and beer. Really stupid but I was a kid with a chip on my shoulder.

I'll never forget the one smart thing Chet ever said to me. We were standing on a busy street corner with cops all around, waiting to sneak into a movie. Chet pulled a blunt from his jacket and lit up.

"Are you crazy? We're going to get busted," I said.

Chet told me to relax. "We're hiding in plain sight. Watch the cops. Who are they harassing? The dudes trying to look small in the corners. They're the ones getting busted. We're hanging out with everyone else." He'd turned to the two girls standing near us and offered them each a hit, which they took. I could lie and tell you we scored with the two hot chicks but in reality we snuck into the theatre, got caught and were tossed out. I don't even remember what movie it was.

My point: sometimes the clue is right in front of you and so obvious you looked past it, so focused on finding hidden meanings and danger around the corner when it was right in front of you.

I still hadn't figured it out but I felt better trying to work through it in my head.

There was a black sports car a half a mile back that had been back a safe distance for several miles. I didn't know if it was following me or the route, but I was still shaking and paranoid so I took the next exit into another gas station.

The black car kept going down the highway.

I was in no hurry right now. I got out and stretched. I decided a snack was in order. I didn't think I'd leave the hotel room once I got there. The flight was super early in the morning to get me back to New York and I had a good hour drive to the airport and the hassle of checking in as well. I wondered if I'd be able to sleep.

Right now chocolate and a Coke was in my plans. Marisa made fun of me for eating convenience store hot dogs smothered in chili but with my diet it was the least of my problems.

I have a sweet tooth and lots of disposable income, which is a very bad combination.

I half-filled a shopping basket with candy bars and Coke until it was heavy carrying it. A couple of bags of chocolate mini-donuts topped me off and I was back on the road and licking my fingers with melting Snickers and Butterfingers.

The black sports car wasn't following me and no one else looked like they were on my tail, either. I kept in the slow lane and just over the speed limit, happy cars were passing me and I was in no rush.

After the first bag of mini-donuts was polished off and half of the candy bars, washed down with two Cokes, I turned on the radio. I found a classic rock station and listened to songs I knew from my childhood or stuff from the 1970's I was familiar with.

My sugar high was getting me to relax and sing along to a Pink Floyd tune I'd never been a huge fan of.

I pulled off the highway towards the hotel, which loomed in the distance. By the time I drove into the parking lot and looked around to make sure no one was watching me, my candy and Coke rush was expired.

I covered my face and cried for awhile.

TEN

I landed back at JFK and was greeted by an older driver with salt and pepper hair, his suit nicely pressed and the driving cap angled on his head like he'd spent an hour with it looking at a mirror. By the steely look in his eyes I knew he was going to be another no-nonsense man like the last one.

I didn't bother asking for his name, either.

My initial thought was to go straight to the jazz club, but I was hungry. I'd spent the rest of yesterday in my hotel room, wiping mini-donut crumbs off my belly and washing down the last of the candy bars with the soda. I was a nervous eater, and when I finally fell asleep with late night talk shows on the television, my stomach was growling.

I wanted a greasy-spoon diner and a greasy burger with greasy fries. I asked the driver if he knew of a good spot.

"I know an excellent one. You want grease? Even the water is greasy," he said and laughed.

I got into the back of the car and checked my phone messages. Marisa had called twice when I was in the air, which is never a good sign.

I called her back, hoping she wouldn't ask me about last night's dinner and she couldn't hear my stomach threatening to riot.

"I got some news, boss, and you aren't going to like it," she said. Cutting right to the chase without small talk is never a good sign.

"I'm all ears." I don't know why I said that all the time to her but I made a mental note to stop it. Yet again.

"I had a guy watching out for Will and he was at the jazz club last night but slipped out the back door. There's an added wrinkle, too: a thug associated with Chenzo is in town as well, and he's been asking questions. I think they figured out the kid isn't dead," Marisa said.

Damn it. The botched job had gotten me behind the eight-ball now. I was a day late and a dollar short, and every other cliché I could think of. I was hoping to be able to work the jazz club and get to Will before anyone else, but it looked like I was going to have to stand in line now.

"How is it possible they know so much already?" I asked.

"I'm not sure. Even Marco has gone quiet to me," Marisa said.

Marco was a tech hacker working for Chenzo's outfit. He was one of the best at getting into any computer system with ease. He loved a challenge. He was the guy who'd told me about the wiretapping by using a common cell phone. He'd helped me out in a pinch quite a few times as long as it didn't interfere with his Chenzo work. I guess now I was getting too close to where he did his business and he was cutting all ties.

"Rumor has it they sent Marco and his buddy Chazz down south after a bad job but Chazz is back in Jersey without the hacker," Marisa said.

This was all getting to be too much for me. There were too many players in motion at once, and this wasn't even my normal job. This was usually much simpler. I got paid to eliminate a child, I kidnapped said child and put him or her through the vast network so they would disappear to live happily ever after in some family that cared about them.

Usually. I remembered Frank Black and wondered again how bad the situation had been for Will growing up, although I had a sneaking suspicion the kid would've been trouble no matter where he ended up.

"I'm trying to stay away from Chenzo as much as possible," I said to Marisa. "If Will vacated the jazz club, what leads do I have?"

"You don't as far as I can see. The guy is in the wind right now."

"Then why am I here?" I asked with anger in my voice. I guess I'd gotten loud because the driver looked back for a second.

"Because I didn't know any of this until you'd already gotten on the flight. Unfortunately, the fortune tellers and soothsayers went on vacation this week and the time machine is in the shop. I'm just doing my job," Marisa said. Putting me in my place.

"Sorry. I didn't sleep well last night," I said.

"I'm sure crying and eating junk food will do that to a man."

I didn't bother correcting her. She knew me so well.

"On top of all this, you've got a few card shows coming up. Just got an e-mail for a big one in St. Louis beginning of the year. I put it on your calendar. And someone is asking about a complete 1960 Topps baseball set. I know you have three but didn't know what kind of prices you were looking at this week," Marisa said.

She'd changed the subject to let me relax and focus on stuff I could control, which I appreciated. Sometimes you needed to pull back and worry about money and baseball cards and nothing important.

"See if he'll bite on sixty percent high book price. Come down no lower than forty, though. All three sets are in great condition but nothing graded." Any graded card was never put into a set and sold individually, except my 1969 Topps cards, which I would never part with.

The car stopped and the driver got out.

"I'm going to get some food in my belly. If anything important happens call me. Otherwise I'll go swing by the jazz club and waste an hour or two," I said.

"You got it, boss."

The driver opened the door and I stood outside a diner that looked like it was last cleaned in the 1950's. I loved the style.

"I'll be right across the street," the driver said.

I nodded and entered and was assaulted with so many delicious smells my stomach roiled again. I couldn't get to an empty table quick enough. Inside was surprisingly clean and bright.

The menu was too much for me since I was so hungry.

By the time the waitress, a pretty young blonde with a plastered smile on her face, came over to take my order I was ready.

"Cheeseburger. Hold the pickle. Add mayo. Order of fries. Order of onion rings. Coke," I said.

"You want cheese on those fries?" she asked.

"If you're going to twist my arm about it… yes," I said, returning her fake smile.

As she walked away I wondered how many old men like me hit on her on a daily basis, and whether she finally smiled at night when she was counting the generous tip money these poor saps gave her. I was going to give her a big tip now out of embarrassment.

The diner was packed. I imagined mostly the working lunch crowd from the area or a few tourist families from Nebraska checking out the sights of the Big Apple.

A television over the counter was set on a cable news channel but I couldn't hear what the talking head was saying. I wondered how big and far this cheerleader killing would get and if the police had already leaked about the white van.

I make it a habit, right after a job, not to worry about reading a newspaper or turning on the TV. If anything major had happened and I was in trouble I figured Marisa would let me know. Back when I'd first started I would spend the next two days changing channels to find an announcement, watching the news for some sliver of information. It was usually a waste of time.

I didn't know off the top of my head how many jobs I'd done and I was too tired to count them right now. I could guess it was close to thirty, though. It might not seem like much but it took a lot out of me each time, before, during and after. Mentally it drains you. The thought of someone wanting a child dead always unnerved me. My mentor taught me a great lesson about this job: the day you felt like you were too old or you didn't care or couldn't cry about what you'd supposedly done was the day you turned it over to someone who cared.

I couldn't argue with his logic.

A glass of Coke, the sides wet with condensation, was placed on the table before me. I thanked the waitress and stared out the window. My driver was in his car and staring across the street at me. I turned away. I was glad for the protection but not being watched so closely. I guess he was just doing his job.

The news anchor was still talking and there was no closed captioning. Even if there was my eyes were getting bad and there was no way I'd be able to read from this distance. I wondered if I was sitting at the counter could I follow along.

A family of four exited, camera around dad's neck even though most people used their phones to take better pictures these days. It was amazing to see some of the prints for sports memorabilia and find out the original shot was with a phone.

My food arrived and I closed my eyes and folded my hands in my lap. I needed to say a quick prayer for the dead girl. I always did. I'm not a religious man but I do believe there's someone upstairs looking over us and I like to give credit where credit is due. It never hurts to cover that base, either.

When I opened my eyes the two thugs were staring at me. They'd just walked into the diner and were doing the casual wander around the room, but I knew they were going to land in the booth with me soon enough.

I just wanted to eat.

A handful of fries were shoved into my mouth and I picked up my burger just as they arrived. They both slid into the booth across from me.

"Can I help you boys? Are you lost?" I asked, taking a bite of my burger and casually looking out the window.

I was not surprised to see my driver had left. Marisa needed to find a new service for me and put the word out this one couldn't be trusted. In this business and most others, reputation was key. Without it you were nothing, and now the dead guy in the trunk had me questioning a few things.

But one crisis at a time.

"Our mutual friend wants to speak with you," the bigger goon said. Don't get me wrong… they were both really big and I had no doubt they could rip me apart without breaking a sweat. They looked like former football players, with no necks and never a smile. They looked like they'd been beaten like a junkyard dog as kids and now a guy like me was going to get the brunt of their bad childhoods and the fact their mama never hugged them.

"Which mutual friend would that be?" I asked around another handful of cheese fries, smiling inside when I saw my hand was shaking. I needed to bust some chops and be as snarky as possible or I'd lose it. I also needed to stall because I knew exactly who they were talking about.

Marisa's *I told you so* was running through my head. Once again she was right. If you never had a face to face meeting with these horrible people they'd never know who you were and try to do horrible things to you.

The other goon leaned forward and scooped up half of my cheese fries remaining. I didn't bother to tell him how rude it was.

I grabbed my burger before his buddy could take it. I was hungry.

"You know who wants to have a word with you," the goon said around my fries in his mouth. He chewed with his mouth open, which I find disgusting.

"I guess it won't matter if I tell you I'm busy today but I can fit a meeting in tomorrow or maybe next Tuesday?"

"Hurry up and finish your burger. Our car is waiting outside," Goon #2 said.

"What about my car?" I asked.

They both smiled. "It drove away for some reason."

"I don't suppose I could hail a cab and follow you?"

"Quit stalling," Goon #1 said. He eyed my burger.

I took a generous bite.

If today was going to be the day I died I wasn't going out hungry.

ELEVEN

They made me pay for my lunch and when I said I had to detour to the restroom they were having none of it. It was worth a try. Neither of them seemed too intelligent, but I guess they were smart enough.

I stepped out onto the sidewalk with the goons flanking me. I felt like a Mob boss and the people walking on the sidewalk gave wide berth to our trio.

"This way," Goon #1 said, pointing down the street. There were several nondescript cars parked and I wondered how many were occupied right now with fellow goons with large guns.

I wasn't going to be able to bluff my way out of this one right now. I really didn't think a sit-down conversation with Chenzo was going to be anything but an end to my life.

I looked both ways down the street, toying with the insane idea of simply running away. Would their size slow them down? Would my age and bad knees even it out? If I bolted there was no turning back. I was a dead man. The innocent don't run away, and I already knew why Chenzo wanted this chat. It wasn't because he was curious about what I knew. It was because, all those many long years ago, he'd entrusted me with killing his kid and I'd failed him. He paid me a huge chunk of money to do this simple task. It was most of the seed money for the sports cards business, too.

Chenzo was going to kill me and bury me somewhere in New Jersey where they'd never find my body. I had no doubt he was going to make this meeting short and simple.

It's crazy when you get older and start to see the end of the line coming closer. Even if I didn't end up in a shallow grave with my face blown off, I was still getting close to the end of the line. It was times like this I was glad I felt so much older and had taken care of a few things.

Marisa gets everything. Plain and simple. She earned it, anyway. If it wasn't for her automating my sports card business online and figuring out everything I needed to do to stay technologically advanced and relevant I'd be lost. Marisa had done it as a whiny teen, too.

As a fourteen year old she'd built the website from scratch and did all the data entry, since I do the two-finger peck typing and I'm not too fast.

In case you're wondering, I was stalling in my own mind. I didn't want to think about what the next move was because I already knew what was about to happen.

The goons hooked my arms and started walking me down the street. I guess they knew there was a very small chance I'd try to run.

I still didn't know which the black cars we were headed to, not that it mattered.

Was Chenzo actually here or would this be one of those long, painfully quiet rides across the river to the swamps of Jersey? I assumed he wanted this more dramatic so he'd be waiting for me at an abandoned warehouse or dilapidated factory somewhere on the Jersey shore with seagulls cawing in the background, finally startled by the gunshot that ended my life.

I'd like to think I had a great run but I still wanted to do stuff. I had a 1969 Topps baseball card collection to complete. Restaurants I hadn't eaten at. Women I hadn't stared at and never talked to.

"If I were you I'd let the boss do all of the talking," Goon #1 said to me.

"I would have no problem switching places with either of you fine gentlemen," I said. I wasn't lying, either.

"Shut up," Goon #2 said.

I wondered why they were even bothering to talk to me. Maybe they knew exactly what was coming. I glanced at both men as we walked. Which of them would be my killer? I knew Chenzo wasn't going to get his hands dirty. When he made the decision to wipe me out it wouldn't be like in bad Mob movies. He wouldn't be tossing the first shovelful of dirt over my rotting corpse.

He'd be sitting poolside sipping a strong adult beverage and one of his cinderblock goons standing across the pool would tap his headset and then nod at Chenzo. It would be done. He could go on with his fabulously illegal life.

A car door down at the end of the line of cars opened and three men stepped out.

It figured they were all the way at the end. More walking for me. They were drawing this out quite dramatically. I'll give Chenzo his props. The kids still say props, right?

The two goons did something odd. They stopped and tightened their grip on my arms.

My eyes aren't what they used to be, so it took me a second to see who was walking towards us and why these goons were now in panic mode.

They both let go of my arms at once and I shrugged like I'd tossed them off. I needed to act like I was in charge of the situation even though it was probably obvious to everyone on the sidewalk with me I wasn't.

Agent Reggie Keane, flanked by two of his own thugs, these wearing the FBI chic black suits and sunglasses, walked up with a grin and a flashing badge.

"Hey, James Gaffney, right? Funny running into you here. Mind if we have a word?" Reggie asked, looking at the two goons on either side of me instead of asking me. I thought it was rude but I wasn't going to tell him right now.

I looked at the two next to me with a smile, slowly moving my head from one to the other. "Actually, I was just going to hang out with these two gentlemen. I'm not sure if we could reschedule?"

The two goons slowly backed away, looking at Keane. Again… no one cared I was standing here, too. They took a wide turn and headed down the sidewalk without looking back or offering a subtle threat in my direction.

They really didn't have to. When Chenzo found out I was intercepted by the Feds en route to see him I was going to really be a dead man. For some reason a guy like Chenzo always looked at things from the worst-case scenario. I was obviously working with the FBI. Keane had painted a target on my back.

"You realize this isn't a good time for me," I said and tried to walk around Keane. His two boys weren't letting me get very far, blocking my path.

"James Gaffney, I am placing you under arrest," Keane said rather loudly.

"On what charges?"

"I don't know. I'll make them up as we go along," he said quietly and spun me around. As he locked the handcuffs on my wrists he casually leaned close to my ear. "Chenzo and his men are a few cars back. They're going to kill you. They know about his son, recently deceased. You've added a complication for Chenzo. He wants to simplify it with a burial. I'd shut up and keep your head down. He might even have the balls to shoot you in broad daylight in my custody."

Great. Out of the frying pan and into the fire for me.

I let the FBI lead me down the sidewalk but I kept my head up. Not out of pride but because if I was shot I wanted to see it coming and know who it was so I could hopefully haunt them as a ghost. Now I hoped ghosts were real.

The goons got into a sedan in the backseat and the car pulled away from the curb, followed by the one behind and in front.

As the last car drove off slowly the back window came down and there sat Chenzo, and he didn't look happy to see me for some reason.

I winked at the Family boss.

The car drove away and I started to shake.

"He's going to kill me. Kill me dead," I said to Keane. "You signed my death notice."

"I saved your life," Keane said.

We got to the last car on the block they'd gotten out of and it looked familiar.

My driver, the old guy who'd abandoned me when trouble showed up, was holding the door open for us. How thoughtful.

"You're fired," I said to the driver.

He smiled and nodded at Keane, who motioned for me to get into the backseat.

I was in the middle between the two FBI agents and Keane went to the front passenger seat, turning around and smiling.

"I'm not as dumb as I look, am I?" Keane said.

"Thankfully. Have you looked in the mirror lately?" I held up the handcuffs. "Are these really necessary? Something isn't kosher about this. Where are the FBI-issue cars? Why is the driver working with you clowns?"

"All will be revealed," Keane said. He glanced at the man on my left and the agent took out a key and uncuffed me. I rubbed my wrists even though they didn't hurt. It seemed like the proper thing to do.

"How long has the FBI been infiltrating car services? Or do you just own the driver?" I asked. When the driver glanced back at me I wanted to lunge up and knock his head off. "In case you didn't hear me the first time: you're fired."

"When we found out you were back in town we made an arrangement with the car service," Keane said.

"He just lost my business."

Keane smiled. "When the word hits the street he had to help us he'll be out of business. An outfit like his relies on getting things done for bad people, no matter what it is."

I thought of the guy in the trunk but wisely kept my mouth shut.

"Where are you taking me?" I asked.

"To a secluded spot where we can talk. Just the two of us," Keane said.

"I've already spent too much time with you this week. Unless we're going to see another ballgame." I sat back and tried to calm my nerves. This had been an intense afternoon so far. I needed to not panic and figure out what was going on.

How much did Keane actually know? He was acting like he'd figured it all out. He was smiling too much, but it could be a bluff.

I needed to take it for a bluff and make this as pleasantly hard as I could for Keane. He wasn't getting anything out of me except my dinner order if it lasted too long.

We sat in silence for awhile and I purposely turned my head and stared out the tinted window. When we drove over to Staten Island I didn't make a sound. I wasn't going to ask where we were going because I wouldn't get an answer and he'd know I was getting antsy.

The car stopped a few minutes later in the middle of a block of typical Staten Island houses, all cramped together and looking the same except for the house paint and the cars in the driveways. The house next to the car was vacant and it looked like construction was underway.

The agents got out and I followed. The two goons stayed behind with the driver – he was still fired in my book – as Keane led me inside the unfinished garage and through a door.

We were in the unfinished kitchen, saws and hammer in sawdust on the counters.

"Are you thinking of buying this place? Want my opinion?" I asked.

"I couldn't afford this cramped box on my salary. You know what they want for them?"

I shook my head. I didn't know and I didn't care. I could never live this close to my neighbors. I'd end up trying to buy the block so I could store baseball cards.

"I'm guessing there's a reason we're here," I said. I wiped off a stepladder and sat down. I looked around, hoping there was something cold to drink and no one hiding anywhere. I didn't take Keane for a guy who'd bring me out to a place to put a bullet in my head, but you never wanted to be wrong and dead.

"I need to know what you know about Chenzo and his dead son," Keane said. He went right to the point, which I appreciated.

I also knew he thought the kid was dead. He hadn't said it ironically or to see if I knew he was still alive. He genuinely thought the body on the beach was Little Chenzo.

"I know about as much as you do. It has nothing to do with me," I said.

"I disagree. Word on the street is he's looking for you, and it has everything to do with his dead son. In fact, I know the two monsters you were walking with. We've been watching them for months. We have enough to lock them both away and throw away the key," Keane said.

"It would've been helpful if you'd already done it. I guess once they take turns beating me into bloody pulp you'll get around to it," I said.

"There's a much bigger picture here, James. You help us put away Chenzo and I won't be so hard on you when we finally catch you doing whatever it is you do. Doesn't that sound fair?"

I shook my head. "You know if I had something juicy, especially on Chenzo, I'd give it over. Self-preservation is very high on my list. But I'm not involved. You're asking the wrong guy."

"The driver said he saw you the other night leaving the airport. Obviously he's an agent and not a driver. He followed you to a suit guy. We questioned him," Keane said.

"Great. Now I'll have to pay full price because you bothered him."

"Here's the interesting thing I need you to clear up for me. We'll get back to Chenzo," Keane said and leaned on the counter although he didn't look comfortable.

"I'm all ears. I'm also getting thirsty."

"How is it the driver you had the other night ended up dead and dumped into the Hudson River an hour after you were dropped off at your hotel?"

I shrugged my shoulders and remained calm. He had nothing on me or we'd be doing this dance in an actual interrogation room.

"We found the car a block away. It had never been returned. Here's the funny part, too. An eyewitness says he saw the guy driving the vehicle that dumped the body into the water and walked away from the car. It wasn't you, obviously. You were already tucked away in your hotel bed. Who was the guy you were with, and which one of you killed the real driver?"

It hit me then. Hard.

The actual driver I'd hired had been in the trunk the entire time. I was being driven around by another player in this game, one I had no idea about. Was he connected to the cheerleader being shot? Did Keane know about it?

I needed to get out of here and think. Think. Think.

TWELVE

"I think it's time I asked for a lawyer," I said to Reggie. It was more about distancing myself from Keane so I could sort through a few things, and I needed to call Marisa as soon as possible.

"This isn't an interrogation. It's just two people having a chat in a house on Staten Island," Reggie said.

It dawned on me what he was trying to say. The rumor for years was Chenzo owned most of the construction, cement and electricians in and out of Staten and Long Island. A few bodies had been dug up every now and then on new construction sites. A few dated back to before Chenzo had gained power, leading everyone to believe his predecessor had shown him the nice spots for the bodies to go six feet under.

"I won't be intimidated by you or anyone else," I said. Was Reggie on the take? Had I underestimated his humanity? Was he on Chenzo's payroll like everyone else? If Keane had a price I needed to eventually find it and get rid of him before he did Chenzo's dirty work and took care of me.

Reggie smiled. "I think you misunderstand me, James. I'm not trying to scare you into helping us. I need you to understand where I'm coming from. Chenzo has his hooks in half the agents under me. There was a shakeup in the Brooklyn office of the U.S. Marshalls this past week. The estimate is half of the agents were on The Family payroll at some point. It makes it hard to get rid of Chenzo or make anything stick. I suspect even my boss as having ties to The Family."

"I still don't get why you're telling me any of this. I don't have ties to Chenzo. In fact, by you pulling me off the street, he'll definitely want me dead," I said.

"I lost your file," Reggie said.

"What file?"

"The eight hundred page folder of everything we've ever gotten on you. Every last sheet is gone," Reggie said.

I shook my head. "I guess you're going to bury me out here in the dumps with the rest of the bodies, is that it, Reggie? After all is said and done, dirty money is more important than doing the right thing?"

"I'm not interested in dirty money for dirty deeds," Keane said. "I really need your help."

"I can't help you and you know it. Why are we wasting time?" I wanted to run out the door but knew his goons would drop me to the pavement. "The two agents with you... can they be trusted?"

"No one can be trusted. It's why we're all alone. I hid your file away. I don't need it, anyway. I've studied your every move for years. When you called me Captain Ahab it wasn't far off. I've obsessed about what you've been doing. Killing innocent children. What kind of man could do it and sleep at night? How could God let it happen?" Reggie asked.

"Are you asking me?"

He shook his head again. "I know you won't give me anything. I get it. Part of the game. I want to crack this case on my own without any hints, James. Then it will be so satisfying for me. The odds are now firmly against me, though. I'm trying to figure out what you're really doing."

"You just accused me of killing children," I said.

Reggie smiled. "And then… a child's body washes onto a beach in Mass. Only, it's nearly twenty years later and he's all grown up. The little boy has been living in secret in another country and the way he got there is really strange. I talked to Sister Patricia."

"I have no idea who that is."

"Yeah, sure you don't. I get it. Again, I'm fine with doing this the hard way and getting to the bottom of what makes you tick and what you're really up to," Reggie said.

"If you know I'm not going to make this easy, why bother with this meeting? Why not just keep following me and see if I slip up. Leave a clue at the scene of a crime," I said.

"I need your help, like I keep saying."

"I don't know how to help you. I'm just trying to live my life," I said. I wasn't lying. I didn't trust Keane because I didn't trust anyone. It was part of the lifestyle, I guess. I was sure someday I'd be able to settle down and retire and find a nice woman who thought I was an old, laidback baseball card collector who got lucky and made some wise investments. I'd never tell her or anyone else what I'd really done all these years. Especially an FBI agent.

"I guess what I'm asking, James... if you get into a corner or find out some information that could help me put away Chenzo, I'd really like to hear it first. Do we understand one another?" Keane asked. He stared at me but it wasn't a lame attempt to be menacing. He was hoping I'd nod my head.

I nodded my head.

"If anyone asks we went back and forth about me trying to get you to confess to all these dead children. That's the reason I took you here, to work you over and get you to loosen your lips," Keane said.

"I'm guessing your goons outside will ask some questions."

Keane nodded. "I don't trust them." He put his hands up. "Let me rephrase that: I know one of them is on the take and it's a fifty-fifty for the other one. They've both been assigned as my shadows by my boss, which looks really fishy to me. But they both know I do some things on my own and they'll sit outside and wait for us to come out. There will be questions, though."

"Not to me, I hope. I'll give them my standard answer I give to all of you FBI thugs... no comment," I said.

I had to admit, this was getting interesting. Chenzo's power was much bigger than I'd thought, and his kid alive had thrust me into the center of a hurricane of hurt. For me.

"I enjoyed the Red Sox game the other night," Keane said and stretched. "I can't remember the last one I'd been to."

"I like to go as much as possible, especially to a new stadium I've never seen," I said.

"How many have you hit so far in your life?"

"Out of the new ones only eighteen. Someday I'll tour the rest. I should be smart about it and find sports card shows happening around home games for places I need to see," I said.

We both started walking towards the door and I knew Keane was making small talk because he was going to do something unpleasant to me before we got to the driveway.

"That would be an excellent goal," Keane said. He stopped in the foyer and glanced out the side glass panel next to the front door. "Those two goons actually obeyed an order and stayed in the car."

"Miracles do happen, right?"

Keane turned to me and nodded. He pulled a pair of black leather gloves from his pocket and slowly put them on.

"Is this where I die?" I asked.

"No. I need you alive. Remember? You're going to help me crack this case and put Chenzo behind bars once and for all. I'll also be able to figure out what you've been up to all these years. Maybe you'll get to share a cell with Chenzo, although I can't imagine you'd enjoy it," Keane said.

"I doubt it."

Keane sighed. "I can't go out there with us smiling and laughing. We've been inside too long. I need to put a mark on you so they see I tried my best to get you to talk."

"You're going to use me for a punching bag? Seriously?" I didn't like this one bit.

"Just one hit to the face."

"I don't think so," I said.

"I need to leave a mark so they can see."

"What if you bust my jaw or damage my eye? I'm not much of a fighter and I bruise easily. I also have a low tolerance for pain. I could go on," I said.

The right cross came suddenly and I had time to close my eyes just as it landed across the side of my head. I was thrown back and banged the other side of my face on the sheetrock. That would also leave a mark.

"At least you didn't break my nose," I said, rubbing both sides of my face. I'd have matching bruises for a few days.

Keane led me outside, still disoriented, and the two FBI goons looked satisfied to see me in pain.

THIRTEEN

I took a cab to Spanish Harlem, walked three blocks before hailing a second cab, and after six blocks took the subway into Manhattan. I was being followed but it was easy to slip by the two FBI guys tailing me once I hit Penn Station.

The FBI on my trail was better than The Family, anyway. I was hoping the agents would scare off Chenzo's men for awhile, until they figured out I was no longer being shadowed.

What bothered me was it wasn't the two agents with Keane. I was being followed by yet another set, and I wondered how far and deep this went with the Feds. I'd suddenly become a person of interest after years of skating by and doing my own thing without interference.

I called Marisa, who seemed happy to hear my voice. Or she had information she couldn't wait to tell me.

"I have some information," she said.

"Shoot," I said. I walked around the outside of Madison Square Garden, trying to keep to the crowds. It was easy to lose yourself with so many different people mashed together on the sidewalk. I also had no real plan for what I was going to do next. I wanted to get to Will Black but if they followed me right to him I'd give it all away.

"I have eyes on Will Black. I've been trying to call you for the last two hours," Marisa said.

"I was hanging out with Keane."

"Is that a good thing?"

I filled her in as quickly as possible on our conversation, stopping briefly to order two hot dogs and a can of Coke from a street vendor. I loved hot dogs and pretzels in Manhattan.

"So you already know the body from the trunk was an FBI agent," Marisa said.

"Way ahead of you."

"Then you also know he has definite ties to Chenzo?"

"Who doesn't at this point?" I asked around a mouthful of hot dog. Have I already mentioned how delicious these are?

"Don't get snarky with me, boss. I'm on your side. Not many people are today, remember?"

I sighed. "Yeah. I remember. Tell me where Will Black is. I'm sick of reacting to everything around me. I need to start acting before The Family, the FBI, someone killing people around me and a really bad driving company gets to me.

My face still hurt where Keane had sucker-punched me and I bought another can of Coke to press against my face and keep the swelling down.

Marisa gave me the address, which was just a train platform where he was panhandling for beer money. Did this guy understand who was after him?

I hailed another cab and when two guys in black suits did the same from down the block I knew I'd been spotted. I climbed into the cab and told the driver to drive as fast as he could around the block, slow enough so I could jump out, and drive to Brooklyn as fast as possible. I handed him a hundred dollar bill, showing him a second one. "I'll leave this one on the seat. Got it? There are bad men following me. If they know I'm not in your cab they'll probably kill you."

"Get out," he said.

I shook my head. "Too late, buddy. This has been set into motion the second I got into the backseat. If you don't hurry the cab they're now in will catch up and they'll start shooting. I hope you don't have a family waiting at home."

I knew I was being a jerk and this guy wasn't in any real danger. Well, if the thugs behind me were mobsters and not FBI, he might be. Those kinds of guys don't really like to leave witnesses.

"You need to drive," I said and pulled a third hundred. "This is all I have. You drive to Brooklyn and get away. Trust me."

He stomped on the gas and cut off another cab, which honked the horn. Cabbie gave him the finger like it was his fault and took off, swerving in and out of traffic.

"They're following," he shouted, his voice hitching.

"Then lose them."

Hadn't I just told Marisa I was going to act instead of react? I was still moving along while outside forces controlled my every move. This was getting old. I was getting old.

At the next light he drove into the intersection even though he had a red light, missed hitting a car by inches, and got into the wrong lane and blew through another red light, turning a corner.

"I lost them," he shouted triumphantly.

"Don't get too cocky. They're professionals. They'll find you," I said. "Slow down."

He pulled to the curb and I jumped out, not bothering to waste time with a long thank you or further instructions. He either made it or he didn't. He knew nothing about me and I'd be long gone.

There was a little boutique and I ran inside, smiling as I turned to look at the junk they were selling in the window. I stepped back so it wasn't obvious from the street I was in here.

A yellow cab went by. Followed by about six dozen more. I had no idea where the bad guys were now. I knew my guy had taken off and I felt sorry for scaring him so much.

I was hoping it was a bumbling FBI cover and once they found his cab empty they'd call their backup to find me. I didn't want to think of The Family members getting their hands on the poor guy. The less people getting hurt because of me the better.

Normally I'd call Marisa to call for a driver so I could escape, but I felt like I no longer had the option. I didn't know who I could trust. Between the FBI and The Family infiltrating everything in New York, I'd need to flush all my contacts and start over.

I had time to kill so I wandered through the store since they sold a few gaudy clothing items on some circular racks in the center of the store. I was by no means a fashion plate but I couldn't imagine anyone in their right mind buying anything here unless it was for a joke or a gag present.

A denim jacket with frayed sleeves and a panther stitched on the back caught my eye and made me laugh. It was so bad it was perfect, and would match my jean shorts. It was actually too big for me, which was amazing. I usually wear between an XL and a 3XL depending on where I'm staying and what great restaurants are in the area. This had to be a five extra large, and I had room.

I found a red baseball cap near the register, added two Snickers bars and a Coke. One thing I loved about New York is the fact you could find pretty much anything and everything if you looked, and not even looked hard. The best part was this outrageously bad outfit would help me blend right in, too. I picked up a pair of cheap women's silver sunglasses, too. Might as well go all in.

By the time I paid for everything with cash and was back on the street, about a half an hour had passed. By now they might've run down the cab and he told them roughly where he'd dumped me. They hopefully wouldn't think I'd still be hanging around shopping.

I got two blocks and saw the guys who'd followed me. They were at the end of the block, peeking into windows and looking pissed. I now took them for definite Chenzo goons and was annoyed the FBI and Chenzo guys looked so similar.

If I changed direction suddenly they'd notice it, so I kept walking, window shopping until I came to a pizza place and strolled inside. I got in line with everyone else and decided if I was going to hide anywhere it might as well be somewhere that smelled this delicious.

I'd eaten pizza in many cities across the country, and you couldn't beat a real New York slice. Seriously. I always tell people, if they travel anywhere near this city, make a stop and have a slice or three.

I stared at the pizza in the display and was deciding what I wanted, making sure I kept my bottle of Coke hidden. Places frowned upon bringing outside food and drink in, which I understood. The candy bars were already in my pocket for future use.

I tilted my head and could see one of the goons stop in the open doorway and look at each person in turn. His gaze stopped at me, lingering too long, before he stepped outside and disappeared.

I was next in line so I ordered two pepperoni slices and bottled water. I figured if I had to run I didn't want a fountain drink splashing around and I could stuff two slices in my mouth while I moved with ease. When you've eaten as much pizza as I have you get good at it.

Marisa once asked me what my dream woman would be like. I told her half-joking she would need to be able to drive a car and eat pizza at the same time.

I took a bite of the too-hot pizza, scalding the roof of my mouth, and stepped to the rear of the dining area, watching the door. I was three bites into my first slice when I saw one of the goons across the street watching the pizza place.

I'd been spotted, even in this ridiculous outfit.

I slipped into the bathroom, stuffing the rest of the first slice into my mouth, and threw the denim jacket and baseball cap into the trash can. I left the sunglasses on the sink and took a deep breath before folding the second slice of pizza and eating it as quickly as I could. I washed it down with half the bottle of water, trying to remain calm.

A splash of water on my face and I was ready. I left the bathroom, expecting to dodge a bullet, and headed for the kitchen.

"Can I help ya?" a young guy making a plate of delicious-looking baked ziti asked as I passed him.

"I'm good. Back door?"

He shook his head. "Go out the front, dude."

"I need the back door. Now," I said, pulling out my wallet. This day was getting way too expensive. I figured another hundred would keep this guy quiet for awhile.

He didn't take the money, looking past me.

When he turned and left the kitchen quickly, I knew I was in trouble.

I was guessing the other goon was behind me, and when the gun was pressed to my back I can't say I was surprised.

FOURTEEN

"Why are we playing hide and seek?" Keane asked and spun me around in the kitchen.

I noticed right away his pistol was still in his hand and his finger too close to the trigger.

"I didn't realize you and I were playing," I said.

Keane finally holstered the pistol and walked to the open doorway to the kitchen.

"We need to go. Chenzo's men will see the cook running out and know there's trouble." Keane turned back to me and smiled. "I saved your life again. That's got to be worth something, right?"

"It would be but you're the reason I keep getting into trouble this week," I said.

"We need to go out the back door. Now," Keane said.

"As soon as you answer a few questions," I said. I still didn't know which side Keane was on and why he was being so cryptic in every meeting we'd had lately. The guy had done a complete turnaround since Will Black/Little Chenzo had come to light.

I needed to know why.

Keane put a hand on his holster and frowned. "Come with me. I'll fill you in on everything I can. I promise. We're wasting time."

I was about to stomp my foot like a child but someone yelled in the pizza place and I didn't need to look back to see what was going on. The goons had figured it out and were heading in our direction.

Once again I was reacting, running out the back door because of things set into motion and out of my control. I was starting to rethink my career choices again.

Yes, like anyone else who's been doing a job for a number of years, I sometimes wanted to stop being in this business. It had a certain stench to it. Even though I never killed a kid, the idea people thought I did was sick and twisted.

Even the constant travel for the sports card business was getting to me as I got older. Marisa kept telling me to stop doing the shows and just worry about the website and mail-order and I'd still be fine. The overhead for storage and shipping was more than enough, but traveling from city to city, shipping in my setups and cards and hotel rooms and food was an added cost. Sure, it was all write-offs when you came right down to it, and it helped me with my taxes and staying on the right side of the law, but it was getting to me. I was getting too old for any of this.

Like running. By the time we got to Keane's car I was winded and slid into the backseat, where I closed my eyes and tried to catch my breath.

"With any luck we can get someplace safe," Keane said as he started the car.

Right on cue the back window was shot out, glass dropping onto my body. I was lucky I wasn't sitting up, or I might have a hole in my head.

Keane screamed in shock before recovering and taking off, the car scraping against the side of the building before he righted us and got onto the street.

I wisely stayed down and the sound of horns honking and tires spinning was enough to let me know to not move.

"At least I know another piece of the puzzle," Keane yelled.

I rolled over onto my back, wiped glass shards from my body, and willed myself not to be curious and peek out the missing back window.

There was gunfire from behind us and Keane cut the steering wheel quickly, throwing me around and slamming my head against the car door.

"I don't suppose you'd be interested in returning fire for us?" Keane asked.

I couldn't tell if he was joking or not.

"Let me guess... your FBI buddies are now trying to kill us," I said.

"That's pretty much what's going on right now. If I can lose them we can get to somewhere safe and put this all together," Keane said.

I slid over but kept my head down, lining up so I could see him in profile.

"What do you have in mind?" I asked. I didn't trust Reggie Keane right now. Too many things were happening too quickly and conveniently for this to be all coincidence. I'd keep my opinions to myself for the time being, though. I still needed to escape from whoever was trying to kill us and Keane was driving. I was going to keep my mouth shut and offer nothing, taking it all in.

"I'm guessing the FBI safe houses are all unsecured in the city and maybe New York State. We need to find somewhere safe to hole up until we figure out what's going on," Keane said.

And there it was.

He wanted me to help him by giving up part of how my operation worked. If I had a safe house somewhere in the area he wanted to go there. Was I being paranoid? Maybe. I didn't want to find out the hard way I was following along with someone playing me. Keane and I had spent way too much time together lately.

"I know a place in New Jersey," I said, regretting it immediately. If Keane was setting me up, making feel like I had to go with the flow and trust him, I might be opening up a big can of worms. If he knew what I was capable of he'd never underestimate me again, and he'd never let me be until he nailed me. Either as a straight-shooting FBI agent and upholder of the law, or as a Chenzo guy who wanted to help bring me down and get in the good graces of The Family.

Either way I was in deep trouble.

"Don't you think Jersey is a little too close for comfort?" Keane asked.

"The last place Chenzo would think to look is in his backyard. But we can't just go there. Can you drive towards Connecticut? If we can get as far as New Haven I can land us a new ride," I said.

"How are you going to do that?"

"I have money, which means I have connections. It also means you need to drop me off once we get there so I can do my thing,' I said.

"No way. You're not leaving my sight."

No one had been shooting for awhile and Keane was still driving like a maniac, so I took a big gamble and sat up. Besides, my neck and back were hurting from being so low in the seat. I turned and looked behind us. For now we weren't being pursued.

How convenient.

"You lost them pretty quickly," I said, trying not to sound sarcastic. I'm not sure if it worked or not.

Keane glanced at me in the rearview mirror and grinned. "I still got it."

I was having my doubts about this setup. The bad guys were coming to get me and Keane rescued me at the last minute, and now we'd hole up in a remote cabin in the woods and over a bottle of scotch I'd cry and tell him all the bad things I'd done in my life before he slapped the cuffs on me.

I causally pulled my cell phone out, made sure it was on mute and texted Marisa. With my lack of skills texting and my giant sausage fingers it took me forever but I got the message to her. She was tracking me already.

I smiled and sat up, leaning forward.

"You planted a bug on me, didn't you? Back in Staten Island? It's the only way you knew my every move," I said.

Keane didn't answer, making pretend driving on the road in a straight line was suddenly worth all of his focus.

I sat back in the seat.

"We need to switch cars. If a cop sees the busted window he'll pull us over. If he calls it in first it will alert the guys after us," Keane said.

I checked my pockets and found a small round disc with a touch of glue. I'd used them a couple of times myself and knew they were expensive but effective.

"How'd you get it on me without my noticing?" I asked, tossing it past Keane and onto the dashboard.

I could see the small grin on his face but he didn't bother to answer.

Marisa was tracking me by my phone. I pulled it from my pocket and called her, smiling when Keane gave me an alarmed look in the rearview mirror.

"Hey, I need a favor. We need a car," I said.

"We?" Marisa asked.

"Keane is driving Mister Gaffney right now. But the vehicle has seen better days. While I do enjoy sitting in the backseat without the rear window and letting the breeze blow through my hair, it is kind of noticeable. I'd appreciate some help," I said.

"He still thinks your name is James Gaffney? Cute."

I winked at Keane when he looked back at me again.

"He's starting to catch up. Not the worry right now. We need a new set of wheels. Something fast but inconspicuous will do," I said. "And not a hybrid. You know I hate the environment."

"You seem to hate everything," Marisa said. I could hear her typing quickly, about eight times faster than I could on my best day. And she wasn't doing it fast, either.

"Not true. I enjoy food."

"We need to get you a pet. You like cats?"

I groaned. We'd been over this a million times already. "I hate cats. I love dogs and goldfish but I travel too much. Any pet would starve to death and then you'd finally see me crying."

"I've seen you cry before," Marisa said. "It's anything but manly."

Keane was listening to every word of the conversation, probably wondering how to break the code we were using. There wasn't any. Marisa and I often chatted about anything and everything. We joked quite a bit and both knew when it was time for business all joking was over.

She also knew I was in a spot right now and needed to get out of it.

"Do you want to stay with Keane or dump him?" Marisa asked.

"I'm not sure yet. What do you have for me in this area?"

"Tell Keane to take the next exit and go right at the light."

I relayed the information.

"Are you sure?" Keane asked.

"Do you want me to help you or no? Just follow the directions so we can get out of this mess." I shook my head and went back to my phone call. "Let me know what to do next so I can relay it."

"Just say the word and the guy at the other end will do you a big favor. For a big fee, of course," Marisa said.

"We just need a good car," I said.

"Suit yourself. Go four blocks and make another right."

I wondered if simply getting rid of Keane would help or hinder me at this point.

FIFTEEN

I didn't let the big bruiser eliminate Keane, even though I could tell he wanted to. Instead, he met us outside, took the keys from Keane and stared at me for direction.

"I just need the car," I said.

He nodded and tossed me a set of keys from his pocket. "Around the street. Black Mustang."

I thanked him. He was a giant of a man, at least six and a half feet tall and with enough prison tats to fill my skin twice. He knew who Keane was and I knew I'd paid more for this car and silence than stepping onto a lot and buying it new, but I needed the car quickly and quietly.

"I'm driving," Keane said.

I smiled and shook my head. "You don't know where we're going. I do. It's time for you to ride shotgun."

"I'd rather stretch out in the backseat," Keane said.

"I really can't argue with the logic," I said as I got into the driver's seat.

"Don't drive too fast."

"You're telling me? You broke a dozen driving laws in the last couple of hours. Sit back and enjoy the ride," I said. I was actually a very cautious driver. Marisa made fun of me because I kept it no more than five miles over the speed limit and always used proper signaling. You never wanted to get noticed and never wanted to have a cop pull you over for a brake light out or failure to use a blinker and nail you for the unconscious kid in the trunk.

I had the same thoughts on tipping in a restaurant: never make a scene. Never send food back, never special order, never flirt too much or be rude with the waitress, and always pay in cash and leave exactly fifteen percent. You never want to be remembered as the cheap guy or the generous tipper.

A few miles later I turned onto a side street and pulled over, watching my mirrors.

"What are you doing?" Keane asked.

"Watching for the bad guys. If we're being tailed they'll stumble upon us. I'd rather have a shootout now. It will do us no good if the safe house is found out," I said.

"When all of this is over, you and I are going to have a long talk," Keane said.

"Agreed. But right now… we hang out and wait. It won't be long if we're being followed," I said and watched. After ten long minutes in silence I started the car. I turned to Keane, sitting in the back seat. "Sit up front. I don't like anyone behind me."

"You don't think they hung back?" Keane asked as he got out and sat in the passenger seat.

I shook my head. "There's no way for them to see us after we made the turn. They'd assume we kept driving and they'd stumble onto us."

"Then what?"

"You shoot them and we continue on our merry way," I said.

"I can't let you shoot anyone."

I smiled. "I don't carry a weapon and when I do it isn't loaded. I'm a pacifist."

"Doubtful. I was about to smack you with the irony of your words and mention dead children, but now I'm beginning to wonder what your game really is. Something isn't right with you," Keane said.

"You're not the first person to say it." I pulled away from the curb, expecting the bad guys to get behind us at any moment. "You do realize, for a single moment when you got out of the car, I toyed with driving away and leaving you behind?"

"Why do you think I made the transition so fast?"

I knew even if we'd ducked them for a little bit, they weren't going to stop looking. If the FBI was involved they'd get state and local police units out looking for us, too. This was going to get really bad before it magically got good for us.

"How'd you get into collecting baseball cards?" Keane asked me.

He wanted to make small talk. I was fine with it. Chit-chat made the time go faster, and if I was being honest with myself, besides Marisa and really bad people, I had no one else to talk to.

The redhead from the card shows came to mind but I pushed the thought away for another, simpler day. Too much going on right now to add a further complication.

"My dad was a huge fan. I grew up in Atlanta. He'd take me to see the Braves, even when they were horrible. It didn't matter whether they won or lost. We had a great time," I said.

I needed to watch every word I was saying because I knew Keane would file it away to get back to my roots somehow. Yeah, I'm still paranoid. I didn't and couldn't trust Keane just yet. I really wanted to but I needed to survive more than anything, and too many guns were aimed at my head right now.

"To be honest, I'm not much of a baseball fan. Too slow for me. I love college football."

"Even though I grew up in the south I never got into college ball. I'm also a big Falcons fan. I root for the home team in all sports," I said. "I collected Braves cards. Dale Murphy, Phil Niekro, Dusty Baker. Great players on bad teams. Niekro made a hundred grand in 1975 for salary. Crazy it was the highest on the team."

"I'm going to guess you make that on a good weekend at a major show," Keane said.

I looked at him, expecting a knowing look or some hint he wanted to talk money, but he was looking out his window.

"I've often wondered if I was in the right line of work. Most days I love it, but there are times I look back through my life and wonder where I went wrong. At what point was the wrong road taken? I was a decent painter as a kid. Watercolors and acrylic, not house painting. A talent. But I was talked into doing something not so creative and common sense." Keane tapped the glass with a finger. "I always wonder if I'd followed my dreams if I'd end up in the same spot, worse or better."

"Why aren't you painting in your free time?"

"What free time?" Keane said too quickly. I knew it was his snap answer whenever he was asked this simple question. He was a guy who had an excuse not to do what he loved and complain about what he was doing instead.

"That's lame," I said.

Keane snorted.

"Seriously. I don't care how many hours you work in a day, you still can find some time. I don't care if I'm collecting frequent flyer miles like I've been doing, I still find time to do the things I am passionate about," I said.

"What's that?"

I knew he was trying to put it back on me and change the subject but I knew I'd turn it back on Keane.

"I actually read quite a bit," I said.

"Anyone can read a book. That isn't being creative," Keane said.

"Exactly. I don't have a creative bone in my body. I'm a collector. I like to hoard sports cards and autographs and books. I have close to a thousand books in my home I'll never get to, but whenever I get a minute I sit down and read something," I said.

"Which home are you referring to?"

Keane was full of questions today. I kept driving and watching for pursuit as we talked.

"You have a gift."

"How do you know? Maybe I'm horrible at painting."

I shook my head and smiled. "It isn't about good or bad. It's about being creative and having an outlet to shut your mind off from the day to day garbage going on. Whenever my brain won't turn off, especially when I have a crisis, I start to read. Slowly I can clear my mind and find I can tackle the issue later. I'm sure, when you're painting, nothing else matters."

"Yeah, you're right. I just need to get back to it. Right now, with all this travel and work, it's hard," Keane said.

"Stop chasing me around the country and go home. Do some paperwork and leave the office at five like you're supposed to," I said.

"I wish it were that easy." Keane stared out the window again, lost in thought.

I needed to find out about Will Black and where he was. I needed to get away from Keane in a way he wouldn't get pissed and come after me even harder, if that were possible.

The rest of the ride to the safe house in New Jersey was uneventful. There was no way anyone had been following us and no suspicious cars lined the street when I pulled into the driveway and then into the enclosed garage.

"Nice place you got here," Keane said as he stretched his legs.

"It's not mine. Just a friends in the event I needed somewhere safe." I hit the button to close the garage door and found the extra key under the mat. I'd never been here before but I wasn't going to give Keane any information if I could help it.

Inside the house was bare; all the rooms empty save a new couch and TV in the living room and a bed in the master bedroom. The kitchen was spotless.

I opened the refrigerator and smiled.

"We have blocks of cheese and a bag of hard salami." I opened the cabinet and found a bottle of wine and a box of Ritz crackers. What else did you need? A knife to cut the cheese, which I found in the drawer with one setting of silverware.

Keane joined me standing at the counter since there wasn't a kitchen table and we ate in silence. Neither of us opened the wine bottle. I wondered if he was sober after the DUI arrest and the ex-wives. I'd never bothered to check if he'd gone into a program for his drinking. I'd underestimated Keane up until the last few days.

"I never thought we'd be hanging out in a strange house sharing cheese and crackers," I said to break the ice.

"Don't forget the salami," he said and shook a piece before shoving it into his mouth.

I pulled two clean coffee cups from the cabinet and filled them with tap water.

"No coffee maker. I hope we're not holed up long," I said. "Luckily, we're in Jersey so there's a Wawa or Dunkin Donuts on every other corner."

"I need to make a phone call. Figure out who I can trust," Keane said.

"So do I."

We finished eating and put everything back where we'd found it.

Keane went back into the garage and I walked into the bedroom and closed the door behind me. We both needed some privacy.

I called Marisa and told her where I was and what I was doing. To say she wasn't happy would be an understatement. I loved her for never beating around the bush, but after five minutes of getting a tongue lashing from her I had to cut Marisa off and remind her who was paying her salary and she was starting to hurt my feelings.

"You don't have any feelings," Marisa said. "What are you going to do with Keane? You can't tag along with him, and he'll only draw heat to you."

"Where's Will Black?" I asked. I needed to figure out one move at a time.

"He is currently in a crack house having a party with a needle."

"Seriously?" This was not getting any easier. I supposed Will Black currently sitting in the room with Marisa playing Go Fish wasn't a likely scenario, although it would help.

"It's actually a good thing. If he doesn't overdose and die in the filth he'll be incapacitated for a few hours, maybe even a day. I'll keep paying for eyes on the crack house. It'll give you time to get back and regroup. As soon as you get rid of your Keane baggage, of course," Marisa said.

"Anything on the cheerleader?" I asked.

"Why?"

She sounded confused, as if it wasn't still my problem.

"I need to figure out who really killed her and what it has to do with me. I need a plane ticket to Las Vegas for tonight. I'm going to have a chat with the person or persons who ordered and paid for the hit," I said.

"No way. You've done stupid things in your life but this might be the biggest yet," Marisa said.

"Again… not asking for your opinion. I need to move and do it fast, before Will Black comes off his high and wanders around with the munchies," I said.

"He's not smoking pot."

"You know what I mean."

"I hope you have an idea about Keane," Marisa said.

"I do. Get this rolling for me, please and thank you. I need to get moving and get on a plane. Give me a two hour lead to get to the airport and check in. I'll need clothes and a hotel room to take a shower when I land, too." I paused. "Marisa, I appreciate everything you do for me. Let me handle this my way so I can sleep at night. I need to get as much done as possible, and sitting around waiting for Will Black to sober up could take hours I'll never get back."

"I accept your almost apology. But I'm not going to stop trying to talk you out of going to Vegas," she said.

I went into the kitchen and looked in the cabinets while I was talking to her.

"What are you doing?" she asked.

"Looking for something… ah, here we go," I said and pulled a heavy frying pan from a cabinet.

Keane walked into the kitchen.

"I think we're good. I've found out who is on Chenzo's payroll and it isn't nearly as bad as I thought. In fact, this actually helps to shake out the cockroaches," Keane said and was smiling until I smashed him in the face with the frying pan.

"Did you…" Marisa said with a chuckle in her voice.

"I told you I'm in a hurry. Call me back when everything's set." I hung up the phone, apologized to Keane and was glad I hadn't broken his nose.

When he came to in a couple of hours and realized I was gone he was going to be really pissed.

SIXTEEN

Against Marisa's vehement protests I flew back to Las Vegas to confront the person or persons who'd contracted me to kill their daughter. I knew I had too much going on right now, including The Family and FBI gunmen aiming at my head, but I needed to keep working. Something about the way the cheerleader had been killed was bugging me, and I thought a face to face with mom or dad would answer a few questions.

Of course, Marisa thought it was taking a huge chance, especially if the dust hadn't yet settled and the police were watching the home or parents. I had to take a chance I'd get some answers and not put myself into the middle of the investigation, although with the way my luck had been the past few days... if I ended up in a jail cell I can't say I'd be surprised.

These jobs are very anonymous for a reason. It makes the person hiring me know I will do my job and not bother them again for a shakedown of future money. It legitimizes an illegal transaction. As bad as it sounds, word of mouth is a major contributor to how the next job comes in.

I know I can't save every child out there. I get it. Sometimes horrible people do horrible things themselves, and there's no way to stop it. Some people hire a friend of a friend with a shady past to do the job, and a child ends up in a ditch or in a shallow grave in a field somewhere. I get it. I can only do what I do and hope I can save as many as possible.

I did a pass in my rental car around the block before deciding the house wasn't being watched. Marisa had pulled all the information she could find from the transaction. The site we use makes the client feel like they've given us no information, but they've given us everything just by using an e-mail address.

Marisa had once taken a month and worked with Marco, who I've mentioned before. He's the premier hacker for The Family. I paid him a lot of money to teach her the basics so her job would be easier. We did it all without Chenzo or anyone else knowing, too. You can never be too safe.

It came into play with this case, as Marisa went back through and figured out who had initially set up the job.

Kelly Osgood. I had no idea if it was a man or woman at first, but Marisa assured me it was the wife. I tried to keep my own feelings at bay and work this like anything else: calm and detached from reality. It wouldn't help me at all to confront a mother and ask why she would want her daughter killed.

I had the paperwork for a bogus insurance claim in hand, one that would get me through the door unless someone wanted to stare at the mumbo jumbo for awhile. Talk of a million dollar policy with scumbags like this would easily get me in.

I knocked on the door and waited, casually looking around for the police, FBI and/or thugs in the bushes. I knew I was getting paranoid again. I needed to lay off the coffee for a few days as my hands were shaking.

The door opened a crack and a small Spanish woman answered with a frown.

I smiled. "I'm here to see Mrs. Osgood." I held up the papers. "I have insurance papers she needs to sign."

"She no here," the woman said and waved a hand, her fingers moving back and forth. "Nails."

"She's getting her nails done? Excellent. Any idea where she went?" I shook the papers again. "This is a lot of money and she'll need to sign this before noon today or she'll have complications."

The woman nodded and disappeared. I was praying she didn't call Kelly, because if Kelly called her lawyer they might see through this charade.

When she returned with a smile and handed me a business card for a nail salon I thanked her. The woman closed the door and I got a fleeting glimpse of her expression, as if she were suddenly very happy.

I'm definitely the guy who sees the glass half empty. Human nature is a horrible thing to see in all its bottom of the barrel modes, and I wanted to kick open the door and smack the maid in the face. She was in on it. I just knew it. She'd helped Kelly in some way to set up the assassination and I was sure this woman would get a few extra dollars in her paycheck once the dust settled.

"Talk to me," I said after programming the GPS on the rental car and calling Marisa.

"Boss, we've got a bigger problem now."

"So, just another day for me?" I sighed and drove wherever the GPS told me to drive. I was getting hungry but needed to wrap this up with Kelly and hopefully do it without a scene.

"I've been hacked," Marisa said.

I held my breath. I had nothing to say. My mind was a jumble of thoughts. Hacked? Is that how the person knew about the cheerleader? Damn. Now I wondered what else they knew.

"Are you still there?" Marisa asked.

I let out the hot air and refrained from punching the steering wheel.

"Whoever did it is good. Really good. Like, Marco good," she said.

"Get in touch with Marco and see what he can find out. Tell him I'll pay him double if he keeps it quiet and works fast," I said.

"Marco is in the wind, remember? Chenzo and his crew are out looking for the guy."

This can't be happening. "Did Marco do this?"

"No. Not his style. He'd have nothing to gain by it, either. If Marco needed something he'd ask me. We have nothing important for whatever he does, which is why he helps us. And the money," Marisa said.

"What did they get?"

"All of it," she said quietly.

"I'm not following you." A knot in my stomach was forming. I wondered if I had ulcers or if I'd soon experience the pain of ulcers.

"Boss... are you sitting?"

"No. I stand when I drive," I said.

"I put everything – everything – into a data base about a year ago. Every job you've done, every contact, every single thing since you started," Marisa said.

"Why would you do that?" I glanced at the steering wheel, which needed a beating right now.

"It was so deeply encrypted I have no idea how anyone knew it existed."

"Anyone online with skills like yours can hack it," I said.

"No. This isn't regular online. This is Deep Web and Tor stuff."

"I have no idea what you're talking about," I admitted.

"Exactly. Only hackers and the government would even know where to begin to look. I tucked our stuff away in such a remote corner it was hard for me to find it some days, and I created it," Marisa said.

"Keane did this."

"The FBI can't even get into where I was. I'm telling you, someone far more methodical and sinister than the government or The Family is behind this. They have all of your information, including who you really are and every child you've moved, and where," Marisa said.

"Wait… you know all of this, too?"

There was a pause on the phone as I pulled into the strip mall for the nail salon.

"Yes," Marisa said quietly. "I know who you really are and who your parents are. I know everything."

"Including who you really are," I said.

"Yes. I really should've told you sooner. I meant to, but I know how mad you get whenever it's brought up. I thought by having all of it in one secure spot I could keep a record for when someone else took over. I was hoping someday it would be me," Marisa said. "I wanted to know what I was working with."

"I'm mad at you. Beyond mad at you," I said.

"Boss, I'm really sorry. If I had any idea this could happen I would've just destroyed everything."

I hung up the phone and punched the steering wheel a few times before I composed myself.

I still had to talk to Kelly, a woman who paid me to kill her teenage daughter.

SEVENTEEN

I find when I'm hungry and feeling lost, the best approach is the straightforward direct route. I entered the hair salon and looked around.

Kelly was seated in the back getting her feet soaked. I recognized her from the picture Marisa had texted to me, or whatever you call it on the phone.

I sat down next to her and smiled.

Kelly did her best to ignore me, closing her eyes and putting her head back as if she suddenly had to take a nap before they got to her toenails.

"Shame what happened to your daughter," I whispered.

She opened her eyes and the anger was replaced by a fake sorrowful look. She nodded her head, sizing me up. I imagine she was wondering what paper or news channel I worked for and wanted to see if I was worth the time giving a blurb to.

"I really don't want to talk about it. Such a tragedy," she said, mimicking my whisper. I imagined she'd done the newscasts all week as well as been on Nancy Grace and anywhere else she could be seen. All for the wrong reasons.

"The real tragedy, of course, is the fact the man you paid to kill her never got a chance to do the job," I said and leaned closer with a smile. "Someone else did the job for me."

Her lips were moving but no words came out. I could see the fear and confusion mixing with her stunned silence.

I patted her arm, making sure it was as condescending as possible. Marisa had already told me what I needed to know and I really should've turned around and gotten onto the next plane out of Vegas, but I needed to do this for my own self-worth.

Kelly Osgood needed to think she hadn't gotten away with this atrocity.

"You see, ma'am, you paid me a large sum of money to kill a teenager in her formative years. A girl you gave birth to? Or was she from an extramarital affair of your husband, or perhaps from yourself?"

She went to leave, her feet splashing in the water. I gripped her arm tightly and squeezed.

"If you move your plastic surgery disaster body another inch I will go public with this. Do you understand? Nod if you do and sit back. Now," I said.

Kelly didn't relax but she pressed back into the chair. When one of the workers came over she waved them off without a word.

"Does your husband know?" I asked.

She turned her head slightly and I couldn't tell if she was grinning or not, but her eyes were sparkling. "Who do you think gave me the cash, huh?"

I thought she'd go through the bogus denial and try to buy me off, but now I could see she wasn't the complete monster I was hoping for. She put her head down and sighed.

"I loved our daughter like she was our own... like she was our flesh and blood," Kelly said quietly. "She was our baby, but we couldn't have her going public with what she knew we'd done."

I wanted to shake her and make her spill her guts but I calmed down and let her formulate the words in her head.

Kelly turned and looked me in the eyes. She was starting to genuinely tear up.

"She was adopted. She figured it out when she was ten. We tried to give her everything she needed. Anything she wanted. We have money and we bought her everything. Maybe it was too much. Who knows? In the end... she knew the family secrets and told a teacher."

"What happened?"

"The man came to our house to confront my husband." Kelly closed her eyes. "He'd been stupid and hadn't told anyone. Yet. My husband took care of the problem. Put the teacher where they'll never find him. Buried in the woods behind the house on our private property. No one suspected a thing. Except our daughter. She knew what we were capable of. What we'd done in the past. What we'd do to keep our secrets in the closet. At any cost."

I wanted to smack the woman in the face. I was beginning to meet more and more people who deserved a beating and I didn't like it. I needed to change my friends if possible. Be around less horrible people, too.

I knew she'd regret telling me all of this, especially so easily. I guess I had a face you wanted to tell secrets to, like a bartender or a priest. I'd missed my callings, I guess.

"Are you going to arrest me?" Kelly asked.

I shrugged and drew out my answer for effect. I wanted her to sweat a little, and I still had no idea why I was really here. I'd never done this before. It went against everything in my code about my work.

"I'm not the cops."

She sighed. "I thought it was like on one of those Investigation Discovery shows, where we paid an undercover cop to kill our daughter and we were going to prison."

"It sounds like you're in prison for it," I said. I put up a hand. "I'm not judging. You're probably a horribly shallow mess to begin with. This is just a blip on the evil in your life and heart, and I wish I was the fly on the wall when you tried unsuccessfully to get into Heaven. You will be judged and you'll burn for everything you've done."

I knew I was slipping into bad territory in my head and I stood to leave and cut this short. I didn't want to be the fire and brimstone preacher, screaming at this sinner to shock her into repenting. Hell, I was going to burn right alongside her for all the bad things I'd done.

He who is without sin cast the first stone and all that jazz...

"Why did you find me?"

"For all the wrong reasons. For my own conscience, I guess. I need to know one thing, though... who was the middle man you used?" I asked, wanting to run out of the nail salon. I knew the workers were waiting for Kelly to give the signal so they could begin working on her nails.

"He said he worked with you. He brokered these deals so they would run smoothly."

"Did he tell you his name?" I asked, which I knew was a long shot.

"Roger something or other. Started with a K, I think. Kelm, maybe?"

I sighed. "Was it Clemens?"

She nodded and snapped a finger. "Yes. That was it. Roger Clemens. My husband said he had the same name as a famous football player."

"Baseball player," I said. First he'd used Nolan Ryan. Now Roger Clemens. Whoever this guy was he was taunting me by also using ballplayers, and especially famous pitchers. He knew too much about me and I didn't like it.

"Any chance he left a number or anything else?" I asked.

She shook her head. "For what it's worth, I chickened out at the last minute. I wanted to get in contact with you – him, I guess – and call it off. We couldn't find a number or e-mail address."

He'd been thorough. I always gave them an out to get in touch and call it off. I didn't judge. Sometimes people made snap decisions they'd regret for the rest of their lives. I wanted to give them an option whenever possible, but the killer had made it so there was no turning back. If I could believe this fake woman sitting next to me.

The killer had left me no clues. I stood, ready to simply walk away from Kelly Osgood and Las Vegas and a dead cheerleader without another word.

"Wait," she said, fear in her voice.

I turned and stared at her. She looked old and haggard under all the plastic surgery and fancy clothes, like someone had put lipstick on a pig and called it pretty.

"Are we done?" she asked.

"What do you mean? Am I going to the cops since you spilled your guts to me? No. You'll never see me again. If you tell your husband about this meeting and he tries to do something foolish, know I will go to the cops." I took out my cell phone and waved it for a second before putting it back in my pocket. "I recorded everything," I lied. "If I don't hear or see another word about this in six months I'll erase it. You have my word."

"Thank you."

I shook my head. "Don't thank me. I didn't do anything today for you. This was all about me and my selfish pride, lady. Someday you'll have to meet your maker and explain to Him what you've done. I don't envy you. Good bye, Mrs. Osgood."

My hands were shaking as I left the nail salon, walked across the parking lot and got into my car. I was away in seconds, pulling haphazardly into traffic and not caring right now.

A crystal-clear thought hit me like a ton of bricks.

I was sure the driver of the car that night was also the killer.

The killer who'd killed the real driver and stuffed him in the trunk.

The killer who took me to buy a suit. Why?

I called Marisa and before she could talk I began going a mile a minute.

"Book me a flight to New York. Within two hours. It doesn't matter the cost. I need to get there as soon as possible. I have to get back to see Jacques, the suit guy. The killer acted like he knew Jacques, and knew exactly where to go. I need to talk to the suit guy," I babbled.

I caught my breath but before I could continue Marisa cleared her throat.

"Boss... I know I'm not your favorite person right now, but I have more bad news."

I pulled over onto the side of the road.

"Will Black didn't go into the crack house to get high. He went in and out the back door. He's gone. In the wind," Marisa said.

"I need a flight to New York," I said and hit the end call button.

EIGHTEEN

I'm sure there are better people out there who don't hold grudges. People who can rise above the petty hurts and forgive and forget when they've been slighted or angered.

I'm not one of them.

When I landed at JFK Airport and got into my rental car I'd missed three calls from Marisa, all on purpose. I really had nothing to say to her. I'd call once I had a chance to talk to Jacques and learn whatever I could from the suitor.

Jacques had come through with half a dozen gorgeous and expensive suits for me and thrown in an extra pant and shirt set for my troubles. I knew he was a legit guy as far as I knew legit guys. I needed to know how he knew the killer.

I also knew I was tired and constantly calling the killer *the killer* was getting annoying, but I didn't have a clue who he was. It irked me. He obviously knew me quite well. He'd hacked into my system and knew every dark thing I'd ever done in my past, and where I'd really come from.

Marisa and I were going to have a nice chat once I cleared all of this mess off my plate, and the anger was propelling me forward. Even though I was really hungry right now.

What did I know? Not much. I hoped Jacques could give me a clue, even if he didn't know the killer personally. If he'd been there before or purchased clothing from him it might help to pick up a trail.

I glanced in my rearview mirror and knew I was being followed.

Great. Just what I needed right now. It was a single driver and it could be anyone: the FBI, Keane, The Family, Chenzo, the killer, Santa Claus or the Tooth Fairy. Any way you sliced it I had another problem on my hands.

So much for stopping for a quick bite, too.

I drove straight towards Jacques' office. No one would figure out where I was headed and I knew I could lose them in a side street at some point. Better to let them think they were still on my trail and I didn't know they were back there.

About four blocks away the car following me turned right and disappeared. I didn't know if it was a good or bad thing.

My phone rang again. It was Marisa. I was going to ignore it but I decided to be the bigger man for a moment and see what happened.

"I've been trying to reach you for hours," Marisa said. She sounded really mad. Not that I blamed her, but I was even madder.

"What's the latest? Chenzo in the middle of setting fire to my baseball cards?"

Yes, I can be a jerk when I want to. Nobody's perfect.

"I've been following Keane all day. He went back to Washington DC to his desk. As far as I know he's been in meetings all day, and naming names. He's threatening to tear down the walls of the place. Lots of rumors flying and an hour ago two agents were taken out in handcuffs. Your buddy is cleaning house. I hope he doesn't hold a grudge like you or we're all in trouble. He'll be the head honcho by the time the day is over," Marisa said. "I spent quite a bit of money with my contacts inside to make sure he didn't slip out the back. So far so good. As far as I can tell, your name isn't being mentioned."

"Thank God for small miracles," I said.

"I managed to shut down our network for now and back everything out. I still have hard copies so I went ahead and corrupted the files and anything they touched. When I get back from DC I'll rebuild it... the network and not the file system. Right now we have no way of getting new clients but at least I stopped him from intercepting any." Marisa sighed. "I know we need to sit down and talk when you get back."

"Yes, we do."

"Until then... I'm doing everything off of my phone and tablet. Once you see Jacques I'd switch over to the next phone, too. As an added precaution," Marisa said.

"I might lose you. I'm pulling into the garage for his building now," I said.

"You could be fifty miles underground and I could hear you like you're next to me. I juice every phone I get. No way I'll lose you," Marisa said.

I was quiet as I found a spot and turned off the car. I was still mad at her.

She finally got the hint when I got out of the car and slammed the door. I knew with her juiced phone she'd hear it.

"Ok… well… let me get back to Keane. Hopefully the guy will stop rolling heads and want to get lunch. I'll stick to him," Marisa said.

"Anything new on Will Black?"

"Nothing. I added three guys to find him. Hit his usual haunts and two goons are on their way to the jazz club to kick in the door if they have to. We'll find him before Chenzo does," Marisa said. She didn't sound too convincing.

"Gotta go," I said curtly.

"Boss…"

I closed my eyes and stopped walking towards the elevator. "Yeah?"

"I messed up. I'm sorry."

I sighed. "We'll straighten all of this out when I finish in New York."

I hung up before we could get into this conversation deeper, which I didn't want to do right now. I needed to focus on Jacques. He hopefully held some answers.

On the ride up the elevator I thought back to the last time I was here and wondered how I'd been so stupid. I took a strange driver's word for it about an attack and the guy in the trunk was the real driver. Why didn't I see it?

I tried to remember as much detail about the driver as I could. I'd never seen him before. He was in his mid-twenties, very non-descript and plain. I guess that was what he was going for. No tattoos, facial scars, crazy goatee or piercings. In movies and TV the bad guy always wore what I call the modern day black hat to set him apart: a teardrop tattoo, maybe a Bible saying on his neck, a shaved head and odd piercings... something to set them apart easily so the common civilian knew they were evil. Real life didn't work this way, though.

A soon as the elevator doors opened I knew something was wrong.

The lights to the hallway were out and the front door to the loft was wide open. Inside was also dark.

I fumbled with my cell phone, silently thanking Marisa for the day she treated me like a child and showed me where some of the basic apps were. I jabbed at the phone, waiting for the doors of the elevator to close or a shot to ring out and wondering why I shouldn't just run and never look back.

Just as the doors began to shut I put my foot out and stopped them.

I found the flashlight app and turned it on. I have to say I was impressed by how much light it gave off.

The light in the elevator was giving me enough light to know there wasn't an immediate threat but if I went into the loft I'd be blind. I grabbed a fake tree in a heavy pot and dragged it to the elevator right before it closed, keeping the doors from shutting and leaving me on the floor. I might need to make an escape, and running down the stairs didn't seem like a fun time.

I knew I was stalling, too. I didn't want to find a dead body or a killer hanging over a dead body. Maybe Jacques tripped a breaker and needed to run out and get a new one?

Four steps into the apartment and I could smell the blood and it was fresh. The place stunk of it and I gagged.

The cell phone light showed about half of the studio, and when I moved a few more feet I saw Jacques.

Lying on the rug in a pool of blood. It looked like his neck had been sliced open with a very thick and sharp blade. When I saw the baseball card of Randy Johnson in his hand I shook my head. As if I didn't already know who'd killed Jacques, he was hammering it home.

Instead of running to the body and examining him for signs of life and getting myself covered in his blood, I continued to shine the light to see who else was hanging around.

The bad thing about having the light so close is the shadows in the corners seem darker, and your mind plays tricks on you.

Plus, when someone steps up to your side and clubs you with something hard, it isn't good, either.

I went down but managed to kick out and hit whoever had attacked me in the kneecap.

The phone almost fell from my hand as I hit the ground but I managed to also roll over and shine the light, already knowing who it was.

The killer.

He smiled at me and now I could see the .22 in his hand. He was still on the carpet near me but if I tried to rise or get at him I'd be shot at close range.

I was beginning to wonder why I didn't carry a gun.

"Mind if I stand? I have bad knees," I said.

When he didn't answer I stood and shined the light away so I could get a good look at his face without being obnoxious and blinding him. He was too far away now to make a lunge for the gun and I didn't feel like getting shot and bleeding out onto the floor.

It was the driver, which again wasn't too hard to figure out. I just needed to know who he was and why he was doing the things he was doing to me.

"I don't suppose you'll tell me your name?" I asked.

"Not my name now. My real name was Harry. Remember me? You kidnapped me from my parents and gave me away to another couple in Portland."

Portland Oregon. Now I really remembered the case.

NINETEEN

"A simple *welcome* would've sufficed," I said.

Harry wasn't laughing.

I tried to think back to the case but it was so long ago. Ten years. Marisa knew more about it than I did. I imagined he wasn't going to let me call her and get a refresher on the case.

"Why did you kill Jacques?" I asked, stalling.

"He knew too much. I've been very careful the last few months to tie up any loose ends," Harry said.

"I'm not sure what's going on but maybe we can go get a drink and talk about it. If I hurt you in any way, I'm sorry. I'd like to make it up to you," I said. I wished I'd had the unloaded gun I sometimes carried so I could at least aim it at him and see how he felt. I was confident the .22 was loaded.

"It doesn't work that way, James. There is no happy ending with us. We're not going to throw a football in the yard together. No baking cookies for old friends. I'm going to kill you and take over the business… and do it the right way," Harry said.

"If you submit a resume I'll look it over, but right now I'm not taking on partners or interns," I said. I was trying to act casual and even managed a smile but I was sweating inside. Had I unwittingly saved a teenager with mental issues, only to have him kill me ten years later as my thanks?

When he'd attacked and I'd fought back I'd inadvertently pushed Harry too far away from me and now I had two choices: rush him or run back to the elevator.

The elevator wasn't really an option. Even if I beat a guy twenty years my junior in a foot race, I still needed to hit the button and wait for the doors to close. He'd probably be shooting me in the face the entire time.

"What if I told you I don't want to die?" I asked. I was actually being honest. I was really enjoying the living and the breathing parts of my day.

"Any last words?"

"How come you sliced his throat but you're going to shoot me?" I asked.

Harry laughed. "I'm going to shoot but not kill you. I want to cut you into a million little pieces and dump you in the Hudson River with the rest of the trash, where they'll never find you."

"All of that sounds tedious. I think you'd thank me for not killing you," I said.

Harry frowned. I could see his eyes, even in the light cast by my phone, and he looked angrier than when we started this chat.

"You made my life a living hell. My parents – my real parents – were coming back for me. They'd made a mistake, and before they could undo what you did they were killed. I grew up poor and alone with abusive step parents who never did anything for me." Harry raised the .22 and I thought he was going to pull the trigger at any second. "I went from being rich to being poor. I could've lived a great life but you took it all away from me."

I shook my head. If I was about to die I at least wanted to get in a few words of my own.

"Your father paid me to kill you. Not take you away and give you to rotten new parents. Death. Don't you get it? Sorry to be blunt, Harry, but your birth parents weren't coming back for you. I met them. They were horrible people who only cared about themselves. You know why they wanted you out of the picture? Because your mother's mother had an inheritance coming up soon and if there was a grandchild, he or she would get six million dollars. Six million reasons to get rid of you," I said.

Harry closed his eyes for a second and that's all I needed. I hoped.

I threw the phone at him with the light still on, marveling at how it spun through the air and lit up parts of the room each microsecond.

By the time it hit him in the shoulder, he'd opened his eyes and panicked, shooting wide.

I slammed into Harry, glad now I was overweight and had about fifty pounds on the guy. Maybe more.

My momentum carried me past Harry, however, and I hit into a mannequin and stumbled, trying to stay on my feet. When I stopped and turned he was spinning on his heels trying to find me in the dark.

I rushed Harry again, and caught him with both arms, trying to drive backwards into a wall or at least the doorway. Instead, we shuffled into the hall and he tripped over the planter I'd used to prop open the elevator.

Two shots as he fell went past my head and I fell to the hallway floor, hoping the doors would close long enough I could run away.

No such luck.

Harry stepped out, holding open the doors right before they closed, and stepped into the hallway with an angered look.

I scrambled to stand but only managed to crawl to the wall and pull myself up in a panicked attempt to not die on the ground.

"I can't wait to have Marisa crying on my shoulder at your funeral," Harry said.

"Stay away from Marisa," I said and managed to pull myself up. I really needed to lose weight and swore to God if I got out of this alive I'd go to the gym. Maybe cut down on the chocolate.

Harry pointed the .22 and pulled the trigger. Nothing happened.

I didn't want to dwell on it too long so I ran at Harry, attempting to barrel him over again. When I slammed into his torso he didn't move more than a few inches, set with his feet apart and waiting for the attack.

My mind went to pro wrestling I'd watched as a kid and wondering what big finishing move I could use to polish Harry off. A body-slam? Super kick to the jaw? Figure four leg-lock? I was losing my mind.

The first blow to my back hurt but I tried to pull back and throw some punches into his stomach and knock the wind out of Harry. At least… that was the plan.

When I moved back he did the same, and connected with my forearm when I threw it up and blocked a blow aimed at my glass jaw.

"Can't we talk about this?" I asked between breaths. There was no way I was this winded this quickly. I added Coke and potato chips to my list of things to swear off if I survived.

Harry wasn't in the mood to talk. He punched me in the side of the head but I nailed him back with a left cross. I guess for all his research he had no clue I was a lefty, but now my one trick was done.

The next blows came in a flurry and I stopped counting at four when I felt my lip and eye split. I'd love to tell you I fought back fiercely and overcame like I was actually in a pro wrestling match and my adrenalin pumped me up to finish the match.

I'd be lying.

You know when you realize too late all those late night fast food drive thru trips haven't been helpful? It all caught up to me in a flash.

"Get up, old man," Harry said.

I tried not to grab my face and will the pain to go away as I looked at Harry. He was bobbing and weaving back and forth like a prize fighter, ready to knock me out in this round.

"Old man? That hurts." I spit blood onto the carpet, at this point hoping the cops would be able to match my DNA when my body turned up in a dumpster somewhere. Hey, looking ahead at this point was a solid move.

Inappropriate jokes and thoughts filled my head to keep me from falling apart and losing what little nerve I had left. I put my hands up and rolled my shoulders to loosen up. And waste time.

"If you've done your research you'll know I've studied karate extensively," I lied.

Harry smiled. "I missed that. See? You learn something new every day. I guess telling you I'm well-versed in *Krav Maga*, arguably the deadliest martial art in the world, won't impress you, then?"

I knew he wasn't lying. I made a mental note to look *Krav Maga* up on Google if I survived and I could still use my fingers.

"I'm a bit impressed. Not going to lie," I said. "I guess there's no way to simply work this out? Shake hands and accept an apology from me? Go grab a beer and laugh about this misunderstanding over a game of darts?"

"Enough stalling. I'm going to enjoy hurting you. If you can feel even a portion of the pain I've felt over the years I'll be satisfied," Harry said.

My mind yelled to charge him again and bring the fight, getting on the offensive before he had time to club me into a bloody pulp.

I stood still, feet planted, hating myself right now. I wasn't a fighter. Heck, at this point I wasn't even a lover. I needed to seriously think about retiring.

Harry had no qualms about fighting, and he took his sweet time coming at me, one step at a time. I wanted to wipe the grin off his face but knew I'd never be able to.

I thought about turning and running down the hallway. I was sure there was a stairwell and freedom, but Harry had youth and weight and speed on his side. The best I could hope for was prolonging the beating.

His first punch was wide and I ducked the other way, easily avoiding it. I realized too late he'd suckered me with his left and his right glanced off the side of my head. That would leave a mark the size of a grapefruit.

I tried in vain to recover but the next two strikes knocked the wind out of me.

Insanely I wished he'd had another bullet left, because I didn't relish the amount and length of pain heading my way.

Just when I thought I'd hit the floor, Harry actually grabbed me by the shirt so he could do more damage to my face. He connected four times in rapid succession, his fist a blur as it bounced off my head. I didn't have time to take stock on what was broken or would never work the same again, but I knew if my nose wasn't broken he'd soon find a way to do it. Both eyes would be black and blue, and my ears were ringing like I'd gone a round with Mike Tyson.

I'm not sure if he was growing bored or tired, but he let go of my shirt and I slumped to the carpet, wanting to close my swollen eyes and take a nap. I was exhausted and I'd really done nothing except take a violent beating. My throat was sore and I hoped it wasn't from screaming like a baby while he was punching me.

"I'm going to finish you," Harry said. He pushed my body over and sat on my torso with a smile. "My face will be the last thing you see in this world."

His next two blows landed squarely on my mouth and I knew he'd broken at least a couple of teeth. They weren't going to heal and grow back, either.

The elevator dinged and Harry stopped pummeling my face.

He swung to punch me in the face again but I managed to turn and the blow only slammed into my ear, which felt like he'd ripped it off.

Harry jumped up and ran down the hallway.

Two hulking masses had stepped out of the elevator and I knew it wasn't Marisa and the National Guard swooping in to save my life.

I closed my eyes and tried to pass out but I was rudely lifted from the carpet, my head swimming.

"Don't die on us just yet. Chenzo wants to have a word with you," one of the goons said.

TWENTY

Chenzo didn't look happy.

I tried to adjust on the chair but the ropes were too tight around my wrists and ankles, and even if I could stand up and stretch I was sure the three goons standing watch wouldn't let me do much.

I needed to figure out how to play this without getting killed. Since getting involved in Chenzo, his long-lost son and Harry, I'd been out of my element.

Pretty bad when your element is kidnapping children and making them disappear. I wasn't built for all this work, and when my stomach growled and one of the goons glanced at me I couldn't help but smile.

"You know you let him go, right?" I asked.

Chenzo looked at his men. "Who's he talking about?"

One of them shrugged his cinder block shoulders. If he had a neck he would've moved it, too. "Some guy was beating him to a pulp."

"He was trying to kill me," I said.

Chenzo grinned. "Then you should be thanking the boys for chasing him off. By the damage on your face he was getting the best of you. I'm a little put off, though… breaking your nose or giving you a black eye would be redundant."

"Maybe you should let me go. I think I've had enough for one day," I said. I genuinely believed it, too.

Chenzo got close to my bloody face and grinned. He had perfect white teeth. I envied him for it right now. My teeth had always been a little yellow from too much coffee, and now a few of them were chipped or loose.

"Oh, don't you worry, Mister Gaffney. There are so many other places on a man's body to hurt. So many bones to break its nearly unfair," Chenzo said.

"I'm trying to come up with something witty to say right now but my face hurts," I said. It did. I didn't know how much more pain I could actually take before I broke.

Instead of beginning the torture, Chenzo pulled over a chair and sat down across from me. Knowing at some point he was going to get up or snap a finger and have one of his goons begin to hurt me was also a form of torture.

"What's the chance, once you're done, we can go upstairs and have a big plate of spaghetti and meatballs? I can't remember the last time I ate," I said.

Chenzo shook his head.

I sighed. They say, in times like this, you see your life flash before your eyes. I'd been in this basic spot a few times now and all I could think about was my grumbling stomach. I think I have an eating problem.

"Whatever you had was your last meal, I'm afraid. I just need some information from you before we end your life. I'm not going to lie: this is going to be painful. You crossed me. You lied to me and you kept this lie perpetuating for many years. I cannot have this. What kind of message would it send through my ranks if the son I thought was killed all those many years ago wasn't dead after all? But now he's gone, right? Washed up on a beach." Chenzo stood. "I missed all of his birthday parties. His Little League games. Teaching my son to ride a bike and how to shave. How to run numbers and fixing a horse race. Things my father taught me."

I decided not to point out the obvious: Chenzo had paid me years ago to kill his son.

"I suppose I should be mad at you for not killing my son. I paid you a lot of money," Chenzo said and began to pace.

He pulled a small pocketknife from his expensive suit pocket and flicked it in his hand. The guy was the walking cliché of a mob boss: Italian suit, soft black leather dress shoes, a pinkie ring and slicked back dyed black hair. Freshly shaven. Eyes like black holes sucking in the light. His smile was pleasantly unfriendly. Chenzo exuded power and fear.

"But… you actually didn't kill my son. My flesh and blood. You gave him another life somewhere else. Did you, in essence, steal from me? I don't like a thief," Chenzo said.

I kept my split lip shut. Pointing out another ironic thing he'd said wasn't going to help my case. *This* guy didn't tolerate a thief? Seriously?

Chenzo stopped pacing and stared at me, the knife moving back and forth in his hands now.

"I'm going to kill you quickly. I've decided. No torture, no fanfare. Would you prefer a bullet to the head or pushed off a building?"

It took me a second to realize he wasn't trying to be funny. He was giving me a choice.

"Honestly, I'd much rather you hugged me until it hurt." I needed to make my play right now before it was too late. "Besides... Little Chenzo isn't dead."

My words slowly sunk in and Chenzo's eyes flickered.

"I know where he is, too." Sort of. "Call my assistant. She's been following him for the past couple of days. Marisa can get your son here. He's in New York last I heard."

"If you're bluffing I will change my offer and punish you for days, one bone at a time. Is that understood?" Chenzo asked.

"I swear. Your boy is alive but scared. I've had him tailed but I was busy getting beaten up by a killer and then your goons – nothing personal – and haven't been able to follow up," I said.

"Where's his phone?" Chenzo asked. One of his men handed it to the boss. He held it up. "I'm going to call your assistant. Put it on speaker phone. If I think you're speaking in any code I'll cut your throat so you can't speak but you can't die just yet."

I simply nodded and hoped against hope Marisa had found Will Black again. If she said she still hadn't located the guy, Chenzo might realize he didn't need me anymore and kill me right here and right now. I needed to do some praying.

Marisa answered on the first ring and when I said hi she got quiet. I never used speaker phone. I didn't really know how, either.

"I need you to listen to me very carefully. I'm hanging out with some friends in Jersey right now. They're inquiring about Will Black… Little Chenzo. They need to know his whereabouts. Right now," I said.

"I have eyes on him, boss," Marisa said.

She'd said boss. She knew my Jersey reference and knew I was in trouble. I hoped she wasn't trying to bluff to save my life, or she'd bring a world of hurt to herself, too.

"I need to know where he is right now," Chenzo said loudly.

Marisa said an address in Weehawken. Will was in New Jersey.

Chenzo pointed at two of his men. "Go get my son and bring him back." He turned to me. "I'm sick of threatening you, so for your sake I hope this is legit. I'll send my men to meet with your watcher and then your team goes away. Got it?"

"I understand," Marisa said. "I'll let them know to keep a visual until your men arrive."

Chenzo stepped behind me and I closed my eyes. He didn't need my help anymore and I was of no further use to him.

When the rope around my wrists was loosened I opened my eyes.

Chenzo smiled at my confused look.

"We're going to have a nice lunch while we wait. You said you wanted spaghetti and meatballs? You won't find it better in any restaurant on the east coast."

His goons led me upstairs.

* * * * *

I'd finished a second massive plate of pasta and sucked up the last of the sauce – Chenzo insisted on calling it gravy but I wasn't going to argue – with the last piece of warm bread when Will Black/Little Chenzo appeared with a smile.

Chenzo and son stared at one another for a long moment, sizing the other up.

"Is it really you?" Chenzo asked.

Will nodded slowly. "Dad?"

Father and son hugged and I admit I got a little teary-eyed at the emotional scene.

"Are you hungry?" Chenzo asked.

"I'm starving. I've been followed for days without a break. I thought the cops were trying to grab me and use me against you," Will said.

Chenzo snapped his fingers and the waitress ran to get more food for the table.

I wondered if now would be the time to thank Chenzo for the meal and excuse myself.

"This is James Gaffney. He helped me find you. It was his men shadowing you these past few days. He knew you were still alive and I am in his debt," Chenzo said.

I stood and shook Will's hand.

The guy had a hand on his dad's shoulder and was grinning. He finally sat down in the booth. Chenzo slid in next to him.

I remained standing, wondering how I should phrase my next question so I didn't end up back downstairs and tied to a chair.

Chenzo looked amused. "Did you enjoy your meal?"

"Delicious." I patted my gut. "After a meal like this you need a nap."

"I'll put the word out," Chenzo said.

Three waitresses came over, pouring wine into empty glasses and putting down another loaf of hot bread. I toyed with the idea of sitting back down and further stuffing myself but didn't think it wise.

I had no idea what word he'd put out or if it was a good thing.

Chenzo saluted me with his wine glass.

"I thank you, Mister Gaffney. I trust this will all remain between us."

"Of course."

"I owe you for finding my son. You owe me for what you've done. I think we call this even," Chenzo said.

"I'm fine with it." I didn't want to ask what I'd done.

"We'll keep in touch. A man with your unique skill-set is a valuable commodity to a man such as myself. Do you understand what I'm saying?" Chenzo asked.

"Very much so." We were even but I was still in his debt and would be doing some bad things for The Family in the near future. I couldn't win.

"I'll have a rental pulled around. Drop it off at the airport on your way out of town. I'll be in touch." Chenzo turned to his smiling son. "We have some catching up to do."

TWENTY-ONE

I was not surprised Keane had found me again. He walked up just as I dropped off the rental car and was making my way to the airport terminal.

I knew by the look on his face I was going to miss my flight. We'd come full circle, and he was out to get me and make my life harder. Missing a plane was going to be a bonus for Keane again.

"Agent Keane. So nice to see you again," I said.

I was glad he was alone. The last time he'd been accompanied by FBI goons they'd wanted to kill me.

He studied my face for way too long and a grin crept into the corners of his mouth.

"I fell down in the shower," I said.

"I had no idea showers had large fists."

"Can I help you, Reggie? I'm trying to get on a flight for home," I said.

"Tell Marisa to call in a new one. I need to go somewhere private and talk with you for a few minutes." Keane held up a manila envelope in his hand. "This might take us awhile."

I doubted it. I knew whatever was in the envelope was just the start of our meeting, and the frying pan to the face was going to be a focus point. I didn't think it prudent to bring up the bruise on his face, though.

Keane led me through the inner workings of the airport, past security which looked like they'd been expecting him. I got an uneasy feeling, waiting to be arrested at any moment.

"Hey, Reggie, I'm sorry about the frying pan," I said lamely.

Keane grunted but kept walking. We ended up in front of a door and Keane opened it and stepped inside.

I followed – what choice did I have at this point? – ready to be thrown to the ground and handcuffed. Instead, it was a small room with only two chairs and an overhead light.

"Have a seat," Reggie said.

I did as I was told.

"Don't you want to offer me a soda or a smoke before you interrogate me?" I asked. I was annoyed I'd miss my flight. I just wanted to get home after the last few days, arrive in Atlanta and get something to eat before an early bedtime. I guess it was too much to ask.

Keane tapped on the envelope but didn't open it.

"I heard you've been a busy man," Keane said. "There's a dead body in a loft in Manhattan. Your blood on the carpet in the hall. Sightings of you with Chenzo's goons and a clandestine meeting of the man in the basement of one of his front restaurants. Yet... here you are. Alive and kicking. It makes a guy wonder."

I leaned forward and smiled through cracked lips and chipped teeth.

"Funny, but I could say the same about you. Stomping around in FBI headquarters with so many of your fellow agents tied into Chenzo and bad dealings. Yet… here you are. Alive and making me miss a flight."

"I put in my notice," Keane said and held my gaze.

I had nothing to say, seriously in shock.

Keane sighed. "I threw everyone under the bus and some of them went down for it. But not all. There are too many agents on the take, and it extends too high up the food chain for me to do any long-lasting good. I knew it was time to get out or they'd force me out. Honestly, I don't know if I can trust anyone right now. I've been put on administrative leave until I retire. I took my pension and gold watch and a shoe box full of memories already."

"This is a setup, right?" There was no way Keane would quit the FBI, unless I'd mistaken him for a different guy all these years.

He shook his head. "I'm done. I'll need to find something else to do."

"Then why are we here? Is this one last attempt to get a full confession from me? Get me to clear your conscience about a few things over the years?" I asked.

He unclasped the envelope.

"This is my one last thing to do for myself. I know I'll never get you to admit whatever it is you really do with these children, but I somehow know it was never as bad as I thought. Especially with what I know now," Keane said and handed it over.

I reluctantly opened it, expecting to find images of me doing horrible things or something I'd have to explain before he arrested me.

Inside the envelope was a sheet of paper and when I pulled it out and stared at it, nothing made much sense. I finally looked up at Keane and furrowed my eyebrows.

"The DNA test came back for the body washed up on the beach in Mass. I was able to intercept it before it became official or anyone else in the FBI saw it," Keane said.

"Any chance you stop being cryptic and tell me what I'm supposed to see?"

Keane pointed down towards the bottom.

"The body found is one hundred percent the real Will Black. Chenzo's son is dead."

"Then who did I meet in the basement of a restaurant?" I asked.

Keane shook his head.

I pulled out my phone and dialed Marisa. While it rang I looked at Keane. "You got plans for this evening?"

Keane shook his head.

"Hello?" Marisa was on the line.

"My traveling plans have been changed. I'll need two tickets to Montreal for today. Right now, if possible. Keane. Yeah, he stopped me as usual. We need to go visit Frank Black again and sort something out. Thanks," I said and disconnected the line.

"I hope you'll pay for my plane ticket. I'm broke," Keane said.

"Gotcha covered. Food as well, I guess."

* * * * *

By the time we landed in Montreal and picked up the rental car, Keane was annoying me to no end. While he was retiring in days, he was still on the job and wouldn't let up.

I'd stopped trying to convince him to keep the information about Will Black in the envelope until we talked to the parents. Going public with it to his bosses or to the media would only complicate things.

Like my life.

Chenzo had Little Chenzo back and all was fine in the world of The Family mob boss. He was allowing me to live and praising me for a job well-done. He was now inadvertently protecting me from anyone who wished to do me harm except Harry. He'd put the word on the street I was under his umbrella, and I have to admit it felt good. It allowed me to breathe easier for a few minutes.

Keane wanted to arrest the imposter and figure out who he really was, but I needed him to catch his breath and relax for a second.

"I'm not sure why we're even in Canada. No matter what the parents say, he's not who he says is," Keane said.

I began driving and refrained from turning the radio on and drowning Reggie out.

"When I met with Frank Black he was all too quick to tell me it wasn't his kid. Without any real prodding. I should've seen there was something not right. He'd been paid off and the wife was also in on it. They're horrible people," I said.

"I can arrest them as part of the conspiracy," Keane said.

"Seriously... I need you to stop talking."

"I have a job to do, James. These people are lying. Someone is impersonating Chenzo's son. I need to pull everyone in for questioning." Keane pulled out his cell phone. "I'll need to contact a friend in the Canadian government so we can cut through all the political red tape. I'll need to arrest the Black husband and wife and extradite them back to the U.S. for questioning."

I grabbed the phone from his hand and stuck it in the side pocket of my car door. I really wanted to throw it and Keane out the window but didn't want to bother.

"What are you doing?" Keane asked, incredulous.

"I'm saving your butt and mine." I picked up speed as I drove. I wanted this over and done with so I could get rid of Keane. "If you shine a light on any of this, you'll get us both killed. What do you think Chenzo will do to the guy when he knows it really isn't his son? When you slap the biggest crime boss in the face to let him know his own kid grew up across the river panhandling and on drugs while Chenzo thought he was dead and out of mind all those years? Chenzo will torture me until I'm dead. Then revive me and kill me again. And again."

Keane didn't say anything but I could tell he was formulating an argument in his head.

"What do you think he'll do to you? He'll burn your life down around you. Ex-wives? Dead. Friends and family? Dead. He'll take Marisa from me, too. I'm responsible for her."

I wanted it to sink in and hoped for the best.

When we arrived at the Black residence I saw the lights were all out and there were no curtains or blinds on the windows.

"I don't like this," I said. We walked up and I knocked. When no one answered right away I looked through the front window. The house was empty. They'd bolted in the middle of the night or they were buried somewhere. Either way it didn't look good for finding them.

Keane shook his head. "I'm going to ask a neighbor what happened."

"Knock yourself out. I'm going to get back in the car and warm up. I'm also getting hungry. Hurry up. I'm done with these people," I said.

As Keane walked to the next house over I called Marisa and told her what we were doing and what we'd found.

"I'll try to research the couple. Maybe they were reported missing? You might want to ask your new best friend Chenzo, too," Marisa said.

"Not funny."

"Oh, but it is. You've received an invitation to go to one of his big charity balls this Friday night. Make sure you trade in the jean shorts for a tux. This is fancy. You're moving up in society. Maybe now you'll date. I can see you all cleaned up and on the arms of a wealthy Park Avenue cougar," Marisa said.

I didn't want to be anywhere near Chenzo, especially if Keane was going to blab and ruin us. I also knew I needed to go. "Obviously let Chenzo know he can expect me."

"Obviously."

There was an awkward pause in the conversation. I watched Keane as he talked with the neighbors.

"Boss… I'm really sorry. As soon as you get home I want to talk to you," Marisa said.

"Yes. I'd like that, too. Where are you now?"

"In Atlanta. I was going to surprise you and pick you up at the airport and buy you dinner. I figured a delicious cheeseburger at Varsity would distract you enough I could really apologize," Marisa said.

"A greasy cheeseburger does sound good." I sighed. "I think I need to eat better. I got my butt handed to me by a guy twenty years younger. I'm always tired and out of breath. I think I'm doing this all wrong, and the last week or so has proven how out of shape I really am."

"I'll clean out your fridge and cabinets. We're going low carb healthy," Marisa said.

"Don't get rid of anything I like."

"You like all of it and it's all bad for you, especially the candy."

"No. Keep some of the M&M's," I said.

"It's all going away. Trust me. You'll thank me for this help."

"I'm already mad at you," I said.

"You can stay mad but be healthy. I think it's a fair trade," Marisa said.

"How about I forgive you now and you don't find the stash of Snickers bars near my recliner?"

Keane returned just as I was done pleading my case about eating the way I liked and Marisa forgetting the stupid thing I'd said about being healthy and living past fifty.

"The Black family sold the house. They gave all their furniture away. Had a massive party for the neighbors, who never really liked the couple, but free food and drink made them tolerable. I'm talking a block party of massive proportions," Keane said.

"They sold the house and blew it on a party?"

Keane shook his head. "They bought a Winnebago. Top of the line. Frank was bragging about paying for it in cash. He said a big family inheritance had come in. They were going to travel the world. I guess he thinks they can drive the Winnebago to Europe."

"Chenzo paid them off. To go away. Thanks for raising his kid all those years. Now they needed to disappear so he could bond with his kid who wasn't really his kid, and the Blacks know it. They got their hush money and what they always wanted: the money is more important than their dead son."

"You know I need to arrest them," Keane said.

"I wish you'd reconsider. Let this play out for a bit. See what Chenzo really does, and let us get somewhere safe or beyond the line of fire. I'm going to beg you if I have to," I said. "Please sleep on it."

We got back into the car for the drive back to the airport.

"I took your advice, by the way," Keane said.

"What advice?"

"I took up painting again. I think I'll spend some time in the Florida Keys and do some painting and fishing for awhile. Spend the few bucks I have on supplies and sleep on the beach," Keane said.

"You don't strike me as a beach bum."

Keane shrugged and stared out the window.

TWENTY-TWO

When Chenzo invited you to a star-studded gala in Manhattan, you went. I didn't want to be here but I really had no choice. It was amazing to see so many movies stars, sports greats and politicians, all rubbing elbows while standing next to a man who had ordered so many deaths over the years.

Power draws people like flies, I guess. It's all out of fear, which is why I was here. I'd finally gotten on his good side and had no intention of being on the other ever again.

I drooled at the spread of foods on the buffet tables, knowing this was going to be a true test. I'd been watching my diet and sworn off junk food and soda. I was eating a lot of filling meat and hadn't had pasta or rice in weeks.

"Don't even look over there," Marisa said.

We'd sorted out our stuff and she'd worked overtime to get everything back on track, and she'd made sure I stuck to my diet and was eating better.

"I'm still mad at you," I said.

She laughed. "No, you're not. You got over it. You'll never get over the bags of M&M's I destroyed, though. I thought your garbage disposal was going to give out."

"Now I really do hate you," I said.

She patted me on the arm. "I'll go and fix you a nice plate of salad."

"By salad you mean the chocolate chips next to the cake?"

Marisa wouldn't even dignify my response with her own, walking away.

I noticed every guy in the place glancing at her. She was a beauty, and the tight red dress she'd insisted on wearing was only getting more looks. I wondered what had happened to the guy she was dating and made a mental note to start asking more personal questions and not just be the boss all the time. Marisa was a good kid and she was entering her twenties with a good head on her shoulders. She was independent and took care of me like I was her annoying dad, which I guess I was by default. We joked all the time but never had a serious conversation unless it was about a job. Maybe she was as lonely as I was? I needed to be her friend and not just her boss.

A waiter offered me a glass of champagne but I declined. I'd sworn off the booze for awhile, too. Not like I had a drinking problem, but I needed to cleanse my temple of toxins.

Marisa's words, not mine. Obviously.

I'd taken a walk this morning. Not a long one, just around the block of the hotel we were staying at. I figured while we were in town for this big bash thrown by Chenzo I might as well keep on my schedule of a few days. I didn't want to tell Marisa, but I was already feeling better. I had more energy and I actually got up out of bed instead of rolling off the side. Even if it was all mental and in my head, it was working.

I felt more alive. I realized each day was ruled by my eating habits. I went through a normal day watching the clock so I could eat a huge breakfast and then figure out how long until a really bad lunch and then off to dinner and then late night snack. Between each meal I also snacked. I had a massive sweet tooth that added to the tire I was carrying around my midsection and it wasn't going to magically disappear.

Harry had easily kicked me around, too. I knew I'd never be in shape to take out a guy twenty years younger, but I could at least hold my own for awhile. If I'd been able to fight back Chenzo's goons would've inadvertently saved my butt.

I was going to lay low for a few weeks and hope another job didn't come in until I was ready again. I was trying to figure out how to get involved in a martial arts class or maybe kickboxing or something physical other than standing on a treadmill at a gym.

Heck, I could buy a gym or add one to one of my houses.

I made a mental note – which I would forget as usual – to contact a personal trainer when I got back to Atlanta. I'd stay in the ATL until the next sports card show and try to enjoy life. Maybe I'd date? Stranger things had happened.

I saw Will Black, or the guy impersonating Will who now went by Chenzo Junior, making the rounds in the crowd. He'd cleaned up nicely, with his thousand dollar suit and new haircut.

The transformation wasn't complete yet, though. His teeth were still messed up a bit and he looked too skinny, but I knew his new daddy was going to fix everything physically about him and try to fix his insides.

"Ahh, Mister Gaffney, so good to see you again," Chenzo Junior said when he finally got to where I was standing. He'd seen me a few minutes ago but thought he was being slick by taking his time. Tonight I had all the time in the world.

"Will… I mean Chenzo… I mean?" I frowned and put a finger to my lips. "I wonder who you really are."

I got straight to the point and I could see I stunned him, which was the intent. I knew I didn't have much time in this crowded room to get my point across, and I needed to nail him and see what his reaction was.

He wasn't too happy.

"Is there a problem?" he finally asked.

"Just an observation from my perspective. I'm just wondering what the game is for you. The end game," I said.

He seemed to relax a bit and shrugged, looking around the room.

"I do what I have to do. Life is one big hustle, right? We've both made my father very happy," he said.

"Who are you? I know the real Will Black, the real son of Chenzo, is in a morgue or buried by now. His father and mother, the Blacks, are currently touring Canada with pockets stuffed with cash. It's all very convenient for you, no?"

It was obvious Keane had kept his mouth shut since we'd been to Montreal and back. I had no idea what his ultimate move was but I had the feeling it wasn't going to be rocking the boat before he retired. He'd done as much as he needed to do to clear his conscience. Opening the can of worms that was this guy wasn't going to make life easier.

"Things happen for a reason," he said quietly and looked like he wanted nothing more than to run away and join the in-crowd.

"Were you friends with the real Will Black?" I asked.

He looked sharply at me and nodded. "Yes. We lived on the streets together. We had each other's back. If it wasn't for Will I'd be long dead. He helped me kick the gear twice. I helped him three times."

"I guess that's what friends are for. I'm really curious how it came down to you killing the guy and dumping him in the ocean?"

He stared off for a few seconds before answering. "He knew who he was. His awful father told him when he was a kid in a drunken rage. Will couldn't take it, and his parents always told him if he tried to contact the guy he'd be killed. Chenzo had paid for his murder. They thought he was dead. He started smoking pot at ten and got into the heavy stuff a couple of years later. Dude was a mess when I met him, and I was a nightmare by then with the drugs. I needed to get out of the lifestyle and off the streets. I begged Will to go see his dad. Get it straight and live the life you were supposed to lead. He wanted nothing from his real old man, who'd paid someone to kill him."

"Paid me," I said.

Chenzo Junior laughed. "Exactly."

"Why'd you save me? You could've kept your mouth shut and let Chenzo bury me," I said.

"Everyone has their place in life. Everyone can be used like in a game of checkers," he said.

"You mean chess."

"I never got into board games. Just using it as an example. I think you're worth a lot more alive than dead right now. I might need to use your skills," Chenzo Junior said.

"I'd never work for you. I'm not a killer for hire, either."

He snapped his fingers. "True. But you are someone with a network for getting things done. You're a guy who has information, which is all the real power today. You can do things I can only dream about."

"I'm not for sale and I don't do favors," I said. I was done talking to this lowlife. He was making me feel dirty just standing next to him. He knew I was tipping my hand because I'd never go to Chenzo with any of this information. I'd be a fool. A dead one, too.

He scooped a glass of champagne off of a tray a waiter was carrying as it went past, threatening to knock the rest to the floor. The waiter wisely didn't protest and was able to right the ship and keep moving.

"Your face is starting to heal," he said.

I put a hand to my lip unconsciously. It had been hard to have anything touch my lips for a couple of days. I was beginning to see the black eyes had gone down from the heavy swelling and my nose as well. Nothing significant had been damaged but my pride.

"I'll be good as new before you know it. I know you're worried about me," I said.

"I was worried one of my biggest assets in the future would be out of commission. I told you, I have a few things I'll need help with. It would be in the best interests of you and my dad to get these things done," he said.

"You don't really want to go this route. I can be quite a gentleman when I have to but don't mistake this smile for a soft heart." I leaned a little closer and winked. "Two Will Blacks washing up on the same beach at different times isn't so hard to imagine."

"I'll be in touch once I get a few things done," he said.

"Like what?" I had to ask.

He grinned. "I'll probably be attending a small memorial service in the next few weeks. I hear the roads in Vancouver are pretty treacherous, especially when you lose control of a Winnebago."

I watched him move away and into the crowd, smiling and laughing like he had no cares in the world. And he didn't.

A part of me wanted to call Keane or find someone in the Canadian police force to warn them about the accident the Black family was going to have soon.

I couldn't be bothered. I know I'm going to burn for it but they also deserved the bed they'd made. I had no sympathy for Frank Black and his horrible wife, and they were going to get what they deserved. I'd learn to live with myself for feeling the way I did.

"I figured I'd give you and Junior some space to talk, but I know you're probably starving," Marisa said. She handed me a plate loaded with meats and a small salad.

I decided to thank her for the food instead of making a snide remark. I really was hungry.

"How long do you plan on staying?" she asked.

"Until Chenzo notices me and smiles or waves. I don't want to talk to him. I just want to get credit for being here. Then we can fly back to Atlanta and relax."

"You know another job will come in as soon as your head hits the pillow in your own house, right?"

I smiled. "Of course. No rest for the wicked."

TWENTY-THREE

I promised myself I'd enjoy the weekend in Miami once the convention doors closed and the sports card show was done for the day. I owed it to myself, right?

It wasn't like I was going to hit the clubs or go down to South Beach and dive into the ocean, but a nice stroll and maybe some window shopping before a sensible dinner and an early bedtime watching Fallon was in the cards.

"Wow. You look great."

I turned to see the redhead and she liked what she was checking out. Me.

"Thanks," I said, breaking eye contact like a fifteen year old. I suddenly became very focused on the cards in the display in front of me, which were already laid out perfectly.

She wasn't good at taking hints or maybe she was done with the brief flirting and wanted to actually talk to me, and hope I talked back.

"How was the Philly show for you?" she asked, leaning on my table across from me. I smelled her perfume and she smelled awesome.

She smelled awesome? Now I felt like a fifteen year old.

"The coast shows are always the best," I said, not making eye contact. I knew if I looked into her gorgeous eyes I'd be a mess.

"Are you doing San Diego again?"

I nodded and made sure the perfectly straight binders to my right were still perfectly straight.

There was an awkward pause and I was too stupid to add something witty, even if my mind could help instead of hinder me.

"Well... good luck today," she finally said and started to walk away.

"Wait," I said, a little too loud. A couple of the other vendors looked up form their work and more than one grinned. I was sure now everyone around us, the regulars we set up nearby during these bigger shows, knew what was going on. I was always the last to know.

She stopped and turned. She was so pretty. Gosh golly, my fifteen year old inside screamed.

"I don't even know your name," I said.

"I'm Dee."

"I'm James."

She laughed. "I know." Her laugh was really nice, too.

"Are you flying right out after the show?" I asked, getting bold and forming actual sentences.

Dee opened her eyes wide before recovering. She shook her head. "My flight back to Myrtle Beach isn't until Sunday night. You?"

"I fly back to Atlanta Sunday night, too," I said, making another mental note to have Marisa change my early Sunday morning flight. This note I would remember.

"Maybe we can get some dinner tonight?" Dee asked.

I was about to protest out of habit but stopped myself. She was upfront and forceful and I really liked it. Why shouldn't I hang out with this pretty lady instead of going right back to the hotel and getting to bed early, before another day of selling cards? I deserved it. I'd earned it.

My face was healing up nicely and I could smile again without too much pain or popping ibuprofen like it was candy. Chalky gross candy.

"Sure. I'd really like that," I said and tried to make eye contact. I made it for a few seconds, until she smiled and her dimples smacked me in my face.

Marisa was going to rip me apart if I told her about any of my feelings, and I couldn't blame her. I wanted to take my man card from my wallet and rip it up and scatter it on the floor. Stomp on it.

"Are you staying nearby?" she asked.

I really didn't want to tell her where I was staying. The Setai on South Beach was over six hundred a night. Marisa had booked it for me, knowing I needed to be pampered for awhile after all I'd been through.

I wanted to get off on the right foot with Dee and trying to explain why a guy selling baseball cards was paying more for a hotel a night than his setup at the show and how much money I'd technically be throwing away this weekend... I didn't need the headache. I also wanted her to like me for me and not because I might be filthy crazy rich.

Did she already know I had money? Is that why she was being flirty?

She must've seen the war going on inside my head because she frowned. "Is everything alright?"

I nodded, wiped the sweat from my forehead, and told myself to suck it up.

I was a man's man. I had my life together. I had more money than everyone in this room combined, and I'd gotten it because of hard work and smart investments. I did something completely illegal and yet completely noble. I'd been around the world and back and seen things most people will never even begin to imagine. I've been in ballrooms with the biggest crime bosses and senators and movie stars. I'd rubbed elbows with some of the richest and worst people in the country.

I was worrying about this beautiful redhead not really liking me?

I knew she did. She'd been trying to talk to me for the last two years at every event. Quite frankly, if I were her I would've given up. I was being the biggest idiot around. I didn't deserve this many chances.

"I'm fine. It's a little warm in here today. I guess I'm getting old," I said and smiled. I stopped what I was doing and concentrated on her face. I was not going to break eye contact. I was better than the weird dude I'd become.

"You're still a young man," Dee said.

"Age is more perspective," I said. I knew it sounded lame and made no sense but she smiled anyway. I was really starting to like her.

"I feel like I'm eighteen most days. I get to travel across the country and sell baseball cards to men who see a woman behind the table and think I don't know the difference between Bryce and Tommy Harper," Dee said.

"Tommy's rookie card doesn't get the prices Bryce's cards do," I said.

"Which is a shame. The buyers chase the next big thing and ignore the stars of yesteryear. We get to mark up prices and sell these guys before they go bust. I have a stack of Brien Taylor rookie cards if you're interested," Dee said.

We both laughed. Taylor had been a monumental bust in 1991 as a can't-miss pitching prospect for the New York Yankees. At his peak his cards were going for huge sums of money.

Dee knew a few things. I was interested to see just how much she really knew about the sports card business and anything else about her.

The announcement came over the PA system the room was about to open.

"Is it a yes or no?" Dee asked.

"What?"

"Dinner, silly."

I nodded. "Of course. You pick the place and I'll meet you there. Sounds like a date."

Sounds like a date? It is a date. Idiot.

"Perfect. I'll ask around. What are you in the mood for? There are a few really good Miami food places not far from here. Interested in eating what the locals eat?"

"Whatever you want. I'm easy."

Dee smiled and walked back to her table. I watched her go and wanted to jump up and down like the fifteen year old I was inside but turned back to my table to get back focused on work.

Just as the first pair of customers reached my table and began perusing the glass display cases and the five thousand count boxes set up on the side tables, my cell phone rang.

"Hey, James… or should I say David?"

I closed my eyes and my hand holding the phone shook.

It was Harry.

"You didn't think I'd forget about you. I'm just getting started," Harry said.

I smiled at the customers and hoped they wouldn't ask me any questions. I looked around for Marisa, who should've been back from getting our breakfast by now. I needed to excuse myself and talk to Harry in private.

"What do you want?" I asked. He had me in an awkward spot right now. Did he know what I was doing? If he'd coincidentally called at this moment he'd soon figure out with all the background noise.

"I want to remind you I'm still looking to collect on payment from you for not killing me all those years ago."

"It was ten years ago. You're being a little dramatic," I said. I decided the best course of action would be to get him so mad he'd screw up. More importantly, I was frustrated he'd called me to begin with. "How did you get this number?"

"The same way I got all of your personal information. The same way I got your address in Atlanta and I spent last night watching your sixty inch television and eating your M&M's. I'm very disappointed you don't have a cat, though. I figured a guy like you, on the wrong side of forty and alone, would have a pet or three," Harry said.

The customer flow was steady but so far no one was looking to break the ice and buy something, which was fine with me.

"I hope you're joking about eating my M&M's," I finally said.

"There aren't any personal pictures anywhere in this house. Nothing with your name on it. The mail doesn't even get delivered here. I can't wait to check out all of your other properties. This is going to be such a fun trip," Harry said.

"I guess you'll bore me to death first?"

"I'm going to make your life a living hell, like you did for me."

"If I did the job I was paid to do we wouldn't be having this conversation. I think I've mentioned this before, but you should be thanking me," I said.

"My life was… unsettling."

"Boo hoo, buddy. Life is bad. Get over it and yourself. I'm sorry your stepparents never hugged you or let you play tee-ball. Don't blame me for it. I'm sick of your generation thinking everyone owes you," I said, suddenly feeling much older than forty-five. If we were talking in front of my house I'd yell for him to get off my lawn, damn kids.

"I'm going to ruin your life like you did mine," Harry whispered angrily.

A guy walked up to the table and asked to see what signed Marlins cards I had. I held up a finger, hoping he would wait a second and not walk off.

"You're like a broken record. You keep repeating yourself. Come up with something new or I'm hanging up," I said. Harry hadn't thought through what he was going to say, obviously I guess he thought he could throw me with a few threats over and over.

Harry laughed.

"I'm hanging up now," I said.

"Before you go, I'd like you to say hi to someone." I heard the phone moving around.

"Boss, ignore this jerk. I'll take care of him myself."

It was Marisa, and it sounded like she'd been crying.

Harry was laughing in the background.

"He's a horrible date, too," Marisa said.

The phone was moved again and Harry was back.

"Do I have your attention now?" Harry asked, sounding oh-so smug.

"Yes," I answered quietly.

There was no way he was in Atlanta. I'd seen Marisa an hour ago when she left for coffee.

"Enjoy your weekend. I'll send you instructions on Sunday night when the show is over. Then the real show can begin," Harry said.

"I swear, if you hurt Marisa in any way I will hurt you ten times as hard," I said.

"Now it's your turn to make idle threats. Nice," Harry said. "Here's the deal: if you go to the cops she's dead. If you pull Keane out of retirement I will cut her into little pieces. If your new friend Chenzo even asks a question about me I will bury Marisa's body where they'll never find her. Do you understand?"

Harry didn't wait for an answer, disconnecting the line and leaving me stunned.

Armand Rosamilia is a New Jersey boy currently living in sunny Florida, where he writes when he's not sleeping. He's happily married to a woman who helps his career and is supportive, which is all he ever wanted in life...

He's written over 150 stories that are currently available, including horror, zombies, contemporary fiction, thrillers and more. His goal is to write a good story and not worry about genre labels.

He runs two very successful podcasts on Project iRadio, too...
Arm Cast: Dead Sexy Horror Podcast - interviewing fellow authors as well as filmmakers, musicians, etc.

Arm N Toof's Dead Time Podcast - with co-host Mark Tufo, the duo interview authors and filmmakers and anyone else they feel like talking to

He also loves to talk in third person... because he's really that cool.

You can find him at http://armandrosamilia.com for not only his latest releases but interviews and guest posts with other authors he likes!

armandrosamilia@gmail.com